"I want to know why you keep rescuing me."

"Maybe I'm just a nice guy."

She stared at him.

"Or not." It burned his stomach to be so close to her. But here he was like a fly unable to resist the lure of the glowing blue light even when it expected the zap.

It's a test, he told himself. He measured his own resolve, his instinct for survival. *Let's see how much willpower I have, what I've learned in the past decade.* He was smarter now and knew enough to protect himself against the pain that Lainey was bound to cause him. Seconds ticked by, and he wasn't sure if the pounding in his ears was his heart or hers.

I can do this.

I can let her go.

Her tongue snaked out and traced the seam of her lip. An involuntary gesture, he knew. But as soon as he saw the pink tip he was a goner.

What the hell, he thought and leaned in to kiss her. Just one time wouldn't mess him up that badly.

Ten years disappeared in the space of an instant. She might look and sound different, but Lainey Morgan tasted exactly the way he remembered.

She tasted like home.

Dear Reader,

I have a pillow embroidered with the quote "My goal in life is to be the sort of person my dog thinks I am." As an animal lover, I think that's a lofty achievement.

Lainey Morgan, the heroine of *Still the One,* has been alone since she fled her hometown after a devastating miscarriage, leaving behind her shattered dreams of being a wife and mother. When she returns to face her past mistakes, I knew she needed the support of a loyal sidekick. In this case, it's a stray dog, Pita, who is devoted even when Lainey doesn't believe she deserves it.

The hero, Ethan Daniels, has cut off emotional ties to anything but the animals he cares for as the town's vet. Turns out the soft spot Ethan has for Lainey's dog also helps him reconnect with the woman who once broke his heart.

I believe in second chances and the power of forgiveness. Lainey and Ethan have much to overcome, but with the help of family, friends and a couple of faithful canines, they'll learn that true love is worth fighting for.

I love to hear from readers. Please visit my website at www.michellemajor.com or email me at michelle@michellemajor.com.

Happy reading!

Michelle Major

STILL THE ONE

MICHELLE MAJOR

HARLEQUIN® SPECIAL EDITION®

Recycling programs
for this product may
not exist in your area.

ISBN-13: 978-0-373-65726-1

STILL THE ONE

Copyright © 2013 by Michelle Major

Printed in U.S.A.

MICHELLE MAJOR

grew up in Ohio, but dreamed of living in the mountains. Soon after graduating with a degree in journalism, she pointed her car west and settled in Colorado. Her life and house are filled with one great husband, two beautiful kids, a few furry pets and several well-behaved reptiles. She's grateful to have found her passion writing stories with happy endings. Michelle loves to hear from her readers at www.michellemajor.com.

To Matt, for believing in my dream.
And to Lana and Annie,
for helping me make it come true.

Chapter One

Lainey Morgan clutched the paper bag, avoiding the corner already stained with grease. "Please," she whispered. "I need this food."

Yanking the sack across the Formica counter, the waitress wagged a finger in Lainey's face. Small sunbursts glinted on the tips of her acrylic nails. "I don't know how it's done where you're from, sweetheart, but around these parts people pay for what they eat."

"I don't have the cash. If you'd let me pay with a credit card—"

When bells above the diner's door jingled, Lainey glanced over her shoulder. At the sight of the man gesturing wildly to a teenage busboy, she inched toward the far wall feeling like she'd been sucker punched. The last thing she needed was to see a familiar face, let alone her ex-fiancé. She knew it had been a mistake to return to her hometown, and just five minutes here proved it.

If possible, ten years had heightened Ethan Daniels's raw appeal. The boy was gone, replaced with a man more suited to the stark desert plains of New Mexico she now called home than this sleepy North Carolina town.

He pointed to the front window and her gaze followed. "No animal should be left in this heat—"

The rush of blood in Lainey's head drowned out his voice.

She needed to get out of the diner. Now.

"You okay, hon?" The waitress had followed her to the end of the counter. "We don't accept plastic for such a small amount. But I guess I can make an exception this once. You look like you could use a decent meal."

She darted a glance at the woman's name tag. "Thank you, Shelly." Adjusting the baseball cap lower, she pushed away the camera around her neck and slid her credit card toward the waitress.

Shelly's voice rang out over the din of the restaurant. "Hey, Doc, what's got you so bothered on a Sunday morning?"

Lainey swallowed hard against the awareness that pricked at her body. Today's agenda did not include puking in front of the weekend rush at Carl's.

"Some fool left their dog roasting in the sun." Heat and frustration rolled off him. "Can I get a cup of water, Shelly? I swear people think two legs and half a brain gives them the right to treat an animal any way they want."

Even angry, Ethan's voice flowed through Lainey like music. The fact he could still affect her after all this time irritated the hell out of her.

"Whose is it?" Shelly asked.

Out of the corner of her eye, Lainey saw a tanned hand settle on the counter. She swallowed hard, praying the floor would swallow her whole.

That prayer, like countless others, went unanswered.

"Can't say." He blew out a breath. "Every canine within

fifty miles has been through the clinic, but I've never seen that mutt."

Lainey scribbled the total plus a hefty tip on the receipt and reached for the bag. The waitress held it tight.

"You know anything about an abandoned dog?"

"She's not abandoned," Lainey muttered. Not yet, she added silently. She gave the bag a hard yank and stumbled when Shelly let go. As an arm reached out to steady her, Lainey looked up into Ethan's dark eyes. Recognition dawned, and with it his gaze filled with anger. Maybe she deserved it, she thought. The way she'd left town ten years ago, why would he show her any kindness now?

"Good lord," he said.

"Nope." Lainey hitched her chin a notch, with the tiny bit of pride she had left. "Just me."

"What are you doing here?"

"My mom—"

"I know about Vera." He ran a hand through thick hair that curled against the collar of his faded Duke T-shirt. "I didn't think you'd come."

"She had a stroke. Of course I came."

"Hold the phone, people." Shelly's heavily lined eyes blinked several times. "Are you…" Glancing at the card before handing it back to Lainey, she said aloud, "Melanie Morgan."

A hush fell over the diner.

Shelly's gaze shifted to Ethan. "She's *the* Lainey Morgan. *Your* Lainey."

A muscle ticked in his jaw. "Not mine," he said. "Just Vera's daughter." A subtle patchwork of lines etched the bronzed skin around his eyes, highlighting their deep chocolate color.

A blush rose to Lainey's cheeks. This was *so* not the way she'd pictured her morning. "I have to get out of here," she said to no one in particular.

"Not so fast, girlie." Shelly leaned across the counter, her twang thicker with every syllable. "Your mama is in a delicate state. She don't need anyone upsetting her."

"I'm here to help," Lainey said through clenched teeth, hating how defensive she sounded.

"Vera Morgan is a saint, I tell you." This from an elderly woman two stools down.

Lainey glanced around the crowded diner. If looks could kill, she'd be a goner a hundred times over. Those angry stares were what had kept her away for so long. And the reason she already regretted returning. Cradling the bag of food against her belly, she raced for the door. To know why people loathed the sight of her didn't make it any easier to stomach.

When the door to Carl's slammed, Ethan blew out a breath. "I need the water to go." He forced an even tone and raised his eyebrows, willing Shelly to remain silent.

She didn't speak. The entire diner was eerily quiet, but the pity in her smile made him grit his teeth. He'd tolerated enough pity for two lifetimes. He'd gone from the town's golden boy to a humiliated laughingstock because of Lainey Morgan and had no intention of repeating that mistake.

He stalked outside where the dog lay under the iron bench. Water sloshed over the side of the cup and dripped down his fingers as she lapped up greedy gulps.

"What are you doing?" Lainey asked behind him. She held a small bowl of water in one hand, balancing the take-out bag in the other arm.

In an instant, her scent surrounded him, different than before—still sweet but with a hint of something he couldn't name. "Shouldn't you be halfway to the county line by now?"

"Not that it matters, but my mother called *me*. Or had Julia call me. I'm not running away."

"We'll see how long that lasts."

"She needs help—"

"I've worked with Vera a long time. I know what she needs." He paused then said, "It's been tough, between the stroke and rehabilitation. She's not used to doing what other people tell her."

"That may be the understatement of the century." She sighed, a small, sad sound.

He pushed his fingers into the thick fur around the dog's neck then looked at Lainey. "No collar," he muttered. "What idiot…"

She crossed and uncrossed her arms over her chest, avoiding his gaze. Finally she reached out and smoothed the hair on top of the animal's head. "I'm the idiot."

Her voice was so quiet he wasn't sure he'd heard right.

"This is my dog. Sort of. Not really." A wave of pink stained her cheeks.

"Your dog?" He looked back and forth between the two. The dog pushed against Lainey's hand as she halfheartedly scratched behind its ears.

"Her name's Pita. For now."

"And you left her in the sun?" He grabbed the blue rope tied to the bench's armrest and worked his fingers against the knot. "Didn't you learn anything from your dad?"

She took a step back as if he'd struck her. Regret flashed through her eyes before they turned steely cold. "I was getting a hamburger for the dog at the diner and her water dish from my car. I'd have been here ten minutes ago if the waitress hadn't insisted I pay cash."

Ethan glanced at the paper bag Lainey still held. "Plus you're feeding her greasy table food. Nice."

Her finger stabbed into his chest. "Excuse me, Dr. Doolittle, but I ran out of dog food and there was nothing off the backwoods highway on my way in this morning." She rolled her eyes. "In case you weren't aware, Piggly Wiggly doesn't open for another hour, and I need to get to the hospital."

She whirled away. Tugging hard on the dog's leash, she stomped toward an ancient Land Cruiser parked near the curb.

He touched her arm but she shrugged him off.

"Lainey, wait…"

She spun back around and shook her finger in his face.

"One more thing before you send the Humane Society after me. I said this dog was *sort of* mine. She's been hanging around my house for a couple weeks. I posted reward signs all over the neighborhood but strays are pretty much the official dog of New Mexico."

She continued wagging the finger and moving toward him until he was flattened against the diner's brick exterior. "She stowed away in the back of my truck—not a peep until the Oklahoma state line. Too late to turn around."

Pausing for a breath, she bit down on her lower lip. Ethan's heart skipped a beat.

Her voice softened and she looked at the dog. "Believe me, Ethan, I am *well* aware I can't even be a decent dog mom."

He didn't understand the sorrow that clouded her gaze. He'd bet the farm it had nothing to do with Pita, who gazed at her with the sort of unabashed adoration only dogs and teenage boys could manage. "I didn't say—"

She flicked her hand. "I've been driving two solid days. I'm going to the hospital and taking the dog with me. If you think I'm that bad, find a good home for her. For now, I'm all she's got."

She stared at him with a mix of defiance and wariness, as if she expected him to challenge her right to the dog.

A breeze kicked up, and she pushed away a curl that escaped her ball cap. Even her face had changed. The soft roundness of youth had given way to high, defined cheekbones and an angled jaw that made her beautiful but not at all the girl he once knew. Her eyes were the same. A color green that turned stormy gray when she was riled up. The same impossibly long lashes.

Memories flooded his mind, almost drowning him with their intensity.

Maybe he'd overreacted about the dog. So what? She wasn't going to make him feel like a jerk. He wasn't the jerk here.

Despite his mistakes, he'd tried to do the right thing. He'd stepped up to marry her, to give her the family he knew she'd wanted. She was the one who'd left him standing at the altar in front of God and most of the damned county. He'd learned his lesson about putting himself out there. About caring too much. Whatever homecoming Lainey got in Brevia, she deserved.

"Good luck, then." He tipped his head and walked past, not trusting himself to speak again. He had to get a hold of himself fast, or this was going to be one long summer.

Lainey didn't watch him go. She didn't need another view of the way the faded jeans he wore hugged his perfect butt. Seeing him bend over the dog had seared that particular image into her mind.

Not that she'd ever truly forgotten.

She bent forward and fiddled with Pita's rope for several beats before glancing over her shoulder. An older couple walked toward her along the sidewalk; otherwise, the street was empty.

Balancing the bag of food on one hip, she opened the back hatch of her SUV. Pita jumped up and plopped onto the navy canvas dog bed Lainey had bought at a pet store outside Memphis.

The dog whined as Lainey opened the paper sack and pulled out two hamburgers, breaking them into pieces over a plastic food dish.

"Look at the mess you've gotten me into." Lainey's fingers trembled as she unscrewed a bottle cap and poured water into another bowl.

When Pita finished the food and water, Lainey piled the two dishes into a corner of the cargo space and closed the hatch. By the time she climbed behind the steering wheel, the dog waited for her, perched on the passenger seat.

"I hope that was worth the trouble." Lainey turned the key and hot air blew from the dash. She sank back against the leather and drew in a ragged breath.

Pita nudged the crook of Lainey's arm.

"Slobber isn't helping." But she reached for the dog, letting the rhythmic petting soothe them both. "Give me a minute to pull it together. I didn't expect…"

What? For the man who broke her heart to be the first person she ran into in Brevia? For the "could have been" chorus to drown out the "for the best" refrain she'd told herself for ten years the very moment she saw him? She shook her head. Enough already. Geez. The dog was not her therapist.

She wasn't strong enough for too many hometown walks down memory lane. From the moment her sister Julia had called three days ago, Lainey hadn't let herself think about anything beyond getting here. Otherwise, she never could have forced her foot onto the gas pedal.

She flipped down the visor and grimaced into the tiny mirror. She'd showered at the dumpy roadside motel, but that was it. She hadn't applied a stitch of makeup or bothered to tame her crazy hair.

Ethan looked better than ever, his body strong and muscular underneath the T-shirt. She'd never been in his league. Why would a decade away change anything?

Pita's tongue flicked her bare arm like a salt lick. "I know. I'm a sweaty mess." Lainey didn't have the energy to push her away. "You act as disgusting as I feel."

Pita barked in response.

Chapter Two

Fifteen minutes later, Lainey pulled into the parking lot of the hospital. As a rule, Lainey avoided hospitals. She brought Pita in with her, needing the distraction and companionship the dog offered. After a quick lecture about the importance of therapy dogs in rehabbing patients and a crisp twenty slipped to the young girl at the desk, she and Pita walked down the narrow hall, the clip of the dog's nails on the linoleum floor the only sound.

The entire building smelled of ammonia and something sweet—like those hard butterscotch candies she'd find buried in her Nana's purse. Lainey climbed the steps to the third floor and stopped at Vera's door. As if sensing something unusual, Pita tugged at her leash. "We're both stuck here," Lainey whispered.

Lainey heard her mother before she saw her. Vera's breath came out in raspy puffs, not quite a snore but in a rhythm that announced sleep. Sunlight filtered through venetian blinds on the other side of the bed.

Lainey approached, her grip tightening on Pita's leash until her nails dug half-moons along the inside of her palm. Vera lay on her back, the left side of her face drooped noticeably and one arm curled at an unnatural angle as it rested on the covers.

Her mother was a force of nature, a whirling dervish who accomplished more before noon than most people did in a week. She looked tiny and frail in the big bed, her skin as pale as the white hospital sheets.

"Oh, Mama." She'd whispered the words but Vera's eyes flew open.

"You came," she began, her voice garbled. Only one side of her mouth moved, and it was an obvious struggle to form the words.

Lainey inched forward, wrapping her fingers around Vera's tightly clenched hand. "I got here as soon as I could." She kissed Vera's sunken cheek, the skin paper-thin against her lips. "Don't talk if it's too hard."

With her good hand, Vera tapped the leash looped across Lainey's palm.

It took her a moment to realize what her mother meant. "I've got a dog. For the moment."

As if on cue, Pita jumped onto the foot of the bed and carefully made her way to Vera's side.

"Pita, off," Lainey said in a harsh whisper.

The dog wasn't huge—blue heeler mixed with more random breeds—but she was no lapdog. Instead of climbing down, she sniffed the covers then curled into a ball, resting her head against Vera's hip.

"Pita, no." But when Lainey pushed at the animal, her mother's good hand swatted at Lainey then settled on Pita's back. She closed her eyes and breathed deeply. The dog sighed and snuggled closer.

Lainey shook her head. Vera's way with animals was legendary. It's what propelled her how-to book on training shelter dogs into a national bestseller. Even Oprah had called for help with a spaniel adopted from a puppy mill raid.

Rescuing and rehabilitating unwanted animals had become her mother's great passion after Lainey's father died. Lainey knew that would be the hardest part of the stroke, putting her work on hold until Vera regained her strength—if she ever did.

They sat in silence as Vera petted Pita. Her voice seemed stronger when she finally spoke, although her speech was still halted. "Good you're here. Need you."

Lainey squeezed her mother's hand. "I'll work on arrangements for your therapy, call the insurance—"

"Adoption fair…"

A trickle of dread rolled down Lainey's spine at the mention of the marquee event the animal shelter hosted each year. "What?"

"So much to do." Vera's eyes fluttered shut and her breath came out in shallow gasps. "I can't…"

Pita whined and Lainey sat up straight. "Mom, calm down. The adoption weekend will be fine. Julia can take over—"

"No." Vera smacked her good hand on the mattress. "Can't do it…baby…need you…"

Lainey reached for the nurse's call button the same moment the door flew open and her sister ran to the far side of the bed. "What did you do?"

"Nothing." Lainey backed up several steps. "She started talking about the adoption fair and went crazy."

Vera prided herself on her "steel magnolia" persona. Her display of fierce emotion complicated things—made her mother seem human. Made Lainey feel responsible.

Julia ran a hand along Vera's arm. "It's okay, Mama. Relax now. I'll explain to her."

Vera's gaze traveled between her two daughters, but Lainey couldn't stop staring at Julia.

Her mouth went dry.

Julia shot her a tentative smile. "You made good time."

"You're pregnant." Lainey's voice came out a frog's croak.

Julia pressed a hand to the mound under her floral sundress. "About seven months now."

"Baby," Vera repeated. "Need you, Lainey."

It was too much. The last time Lainey had been in this hospital, she'd been the pregnant one. Only one floor up was the room where she'd lost her baby. Ethan's baby. Where complications from the miscarriage had changed her life forever. Lainey forced her gaze back to her mother. "What is it you want, Mom?"

Vera looked at Julia, who nodded and turned to Lainey. "Most of the plans for 'Paws for the Cause' are in place. Loose ends need to be tied up, sponsor and press stuff, getting the site ready. I can help, but I'm having issues with preterm labor. If I don't take it easy I'll be on bed rest."

Lainey's mind raced as she tried to absorb Julia's exact meaning. "Why didn't you tell me you were pregnant? Did you think I wouldn't come?"

Julia shook her head. "It wasn't like that. When I called about Mom it had been ages since we'd spoken."

"Ten years." *Not long enough to make this reunion any easier.*

"Right. So it didn't seem like the best time to fill you in on my life, you know?"

Lainey did know, but that didn't lessen her shock. "The shelter event is when?" she asked, trying to focus on the topic at hand.

"September 15."

"That's over a month from now." She paced the room. "I can't stay for six weeks. I have an assignment at the end of the month." The thought of being in one place—in this place— for the entire summer had her stomach clenching.

"I need you," Vera repeated. "We all need you."

Lainey focused her attention on Pita, still resting next to her mother. The dog met her gaze and cocked its head as if to say, "If you bolt, I'm coming, too."

Julia leaned forward across the bed. "Are you okay?"

Lainey was many things, but "okay" didn't top the list. "You were trying for a baby? Mom never said…"

"I wasn't." A tiny crease marred Julia's smooth brow. "Not exactly. I'm kind of putting the cart before the horse, but Jeff and I will get married as soon as his work settles down."

She'd never met Julia's anthropology professor boyfriend, but the reports Vera had insisted on giving her over the past three years hadn't been positive. She knew it wasn't right to pick a fight just so she could channel her mixed-up emotions, but it didn't stop her. "Too busy for a wedding," she answered slowly. "Sure, I get it."

Julia's shoulders stiffened, but to Lainey's shock she didn't come out swinging. "The baby is a surprise, but a welcome one. It just sort of…happened."

Right. Just happened. Since childhood, everything in life had come easy for her sister—friends, grades, their parents' approval. Ethan Daniels falling in love with Julia as Lainey, nursing a wicked crush on him, watched from the shadows. Why should a baby be different?

"I can't blow off my assignment…" she began.

Vera shook her head, the movement jerky. "You stay here. This is for Dad, his memory. Need you, Melanie."

Lainey stared at her mother, wondering how she knew the exact thing to say to cut into Lainey's well-guarded heart. A million excuses ran through her mind. A thousand rationales why she should walk out and not look back.

She knew what it meant to take this on but understood the shame of leaving even better. The last time she'd left Brevia had been her wedding day. When she couldn't bear the thought of marrying a man she knew didn't love her. Of never being able to have the family she'd craved since childhood. Yes, Lainey had run away once. Made a career of circling the globe in search of the perfect photo, the constant travel required of her job helping her to pretend her life had purpose.

Her mother met her gaze. The silence stretched so long Julia finally broke it. "If you can't get the time off, I'm sure I'll be able to—"

"I'll stay."

Lainey wondered what this decision would cost her emotionally. How long it would take her to get her life back on track. But she couldn't say no to Vera. Lainey's relationship with Ethan had torn her family apart, and this might be her only chance to mend fences. She had no choice but to try.

A lopsided smile stretched across her mother's face. She reached out and placed her hand on top of Lainey's. *Here comes the emotion, the gratitude.* She would stay, but she wouldn't let herself get emotionally involved. This was a final payment for past mistakes, she told herself. Nothing more. Lainey ratcheted up her mental defenses at the same time the little girl inside her waited anxiously.

"Get coffee," her mother said. "You look tired. Lots of work now."

Lainey shook her head. So much for the tender reunion.

Wasn't that typical and one heck of a welcome home.

Lainey climbed the back porch steps of her mother's house later that night. Pita sniffed the rosebushes that ran the length of the house.

"You can't imagine how much I don't want to be here."

The dog nudged her nose into Lainey's knee.

"Please don't pee in Vera's garden. She'll kill us both."

She paused at the top, running one hand over the white-washed post. How many times had she come tearing out of the house for the woods around back, hand sliding along the railing so she didn't lose her balance?

Too many to count. She'd felt at peace exploring the thick underbrush of the forest—as much of a loner then as she was now. Things were easier that way, not so much mess.

The sky took on a pinkish cast at twilight. A brief summer storm had blown in a few hours earlier, tempering the blazing heat but sending the humidity so high she could practically see the cloud of thick air that surrounded her.

As a photojournalist, she'd traveled all over the world, from Antarctica to some of the thickest jungles of the Amazon. Nothing overwhelmed her senses like a summer night in North Carolina.

Shaking off nostalgia, she reached for the door. Through the four-pane window she saw a man seated at the old trestle table, his large hands cradling the rounded belly of the woman in front of him: Julia.

Her heart thundered in her chest as memories and long-buried pain rushed in.

Ethan had no way of knowing Lainey had been in love with him since she was barely more than a girl. He'd started dating Julia in high school and they'd been Brevia's perfect couple. Everyone had been shocked when Julia left for New York during Ethan's first year of med school, taking her big dreams and his heart with her.

Devastated, he'd turned to Lainey, who was at the same university campus, as a friend. Very quickly it led to more, and Lainey couldn't resist—being in Ethan's arms made her feel like all her dreams were coming true.

She'd thought it was safe because her sister had ended things and moved on with her life. Only when Lainey had become pregnant a few months later and Julia returned to re-kindle her relationship with Ethan did Lainey see how stupid and selfish she'd been. It didn't matter that Julia and Ethan had been broken up or that Lainey had secretly loved him for years. She should never have given in to her heart.

All hell had broken loose in their family as Ethan chose his duty to Lainey over his history with her sister. Ultimately, Lainey's love story was still doomed.

Julia had left town again after finding out Lainey was pregnant with Ethan's baby. She had no idea what Lainey had lost or the emotional and physical pain she'd suffered.

Lainey thought she'd gotten over the sorrow, but the image in front of her was exactly what she'd imagined for herself. To watch the moment unfold between Julia and Ethan was simply too much. She threw open the door.

Pita scampered over to Ethan, resting her head against his thigh. Lainey narrowed her eyes at the unfaithful mutt.

"Sorry to interrupt…"

"You didn't." Julia moved to the far end of the kitchen. "The baby's active. I wanted Ethan—someone—to feel how hard he kicks." She stepped closer. "You want to try?"

Lainey backed against the doorframe like Julia had pulled a knife on her. "No!" Her hands shook and she crossed her arms over her chest. "Not now. It's been a long day."

"Sure, I understand." Julia looked confused but busied herself with arranging a bowl of apples on the center island. "How was Mom when you left?"

"Sleeping."

"She's happy you're here." Julia laughed without humor. "She hated the idea that I'd try to run the adoption fair and screw it up."

Before Lainey could answer, Ethan's chair scraped on the wood floor. "Do you have bags in the car? I'll bring them in."

"It's unlocked."

As he stepped past her out the back door, she came farther into the kitchen, walking back in time. The walls were painted the same warm yellow she remembered, and a short valance with bright red cherries hung from the bank of windows framing the breakfast nook.

She faced Julia across the large island. "What are you two doing here?" she whispered, glancing over her shoulder.

"I picked up groceries." Julia held up an apple. "Vera's command. Keep you well fed and you'll have more energy to do her bidding." She arched one brow. "Ethan was in the driveway when I got here. Maybe he was waiting for you."

"Doubtful. He ripped my head off this morning at Carl's."

Julia's big eyes widened farther. "You'd seen him before you got to the hospital? That was quick, even for you."

Ouch. The comment stung although she understood the insinuation behind it. Julia had only been gone a couple of months before Lainey and Ethan had begun their brief relationship. But when you'd loved someone forever the way Lainey had loved Ethan, timing didn't matter the same way.

At least it hadn't to her. Now she knew better.

"I never wanted to come back."

Julia put away a gallon of milk and moved a box of Cheerios to the back of the counter. "We're adults now. We can make it work."

Unconvinced, Lainey nodded, willing the words to be true. "Did Mom command you to say that?"

Julia sighed. "Maybe."

Ethan's heavy footfalls sounded on the porch. "Where do you want these?" he asked as he came through the back door carrying two large suitcases.

"In my old room. First one on the left."

"I know which room is yours," he mumbled under his breath.

Right.

She watched him maneuver the luggage through the doorway and down the narrow hall that led to the stairs. Muscles bunched under his T-shirt as he hefted the larger bag over the table in the entry.

Julia studied her with an unreadable expression.

"What?"

Julia raised her hands, palms facing forward. "Nothing at all, Lain-Brain," she said.

"Don't call me that. It was awful when I was ten. Now it's downright rude."

Julia walked around the side of the island. "I'll see you at the hospital in the morning. Visiting hours start at eight."

"You can't leave," Lainey whispered. "Shouldn't you and Ethan walk out together?"

Julia shook her head. "I don't think so. He wasn't lurking around the garage for me."

"Do not go…"

Julia's pace didn't slow. "The question is does the nickname still fit?" she called over her shoulder.

"Julia!"

"Is there anything else I can bring in?"

She whirled at the sound of Ethan's voice. He filled the doorway between the hall and the kitchen, a lock of hair falling across his dark eyes.

Once upon a time, she'd spent hours gazing at him, memorizing every bit of his face. Now she only wanted to forget. She tried to muster the anger she'd felt that morning but couldn't find the energy for it.

"I don't think so." She wrapped her arms tighter around herself. "Just so you know, I got dog food."

"I left a couple bags in the garage, too."

"Excuse me?"

He stepped toward her then stopped and ran one hand through his hair, the same unconscious gesture he'd had since high school. "It's important to Vera that you came. Buying a bag of kibble is easier than giving you grief about what you feed your dog."

She could deal with anger from him, but not kindness. Kindness might melt her frozen heart, and Lainey couldn't risk the heartbreak again. "Like I told you, she's not exactly *my* dog."

When he didn't respond, she walked to the counter to continue unloading groceries. "So if you know of anyone who needs a new pet…"

"How long are you staying?"

Her hands stilled on a bag of mini-carrots. "Mom wants me to run the entire adoption fair."

He nodded. "I figured as much. That weekend means the world to her."

Lainey laughed. "Then it's hard to believe she'd trust it with me. We'll see. I've got a couple assignments I need to reschedule. A summer in Brevia wasn't part of the plan."

He rocked back on his heels. "I saw your feature in *Outside Magazine* on the volcanoes. And the pictures of Everest from *National Geographic*. Amazing."

Never in a million years could Lainey have imagined this conversation. The life of a nomadic photographer was so different than the future she'd planned it was almost comical. But she knew Vera paraded the magazines with her pictorials by anyone who crossed her path.

Even though she shot for a number of national publications, every picture was personal. She put a piece of her soul into each photo and it made her uncomfortable knowing Ethan had seen them. Even stranger that he actually remembered her spreads.

She couldn't put into words the way traveling had saved her, allowed her to escape from her mind and the constant pain of losing her baby and the man she'd loved. She hadn't been able to talk about the tragedy ten years ago, and she certainly wouldn't now. Instead she told him, "I'm lucky to have the job I do."

He watched her for several seconds like he'd forgotten what she'd just said. "That's cool," he answered finally.

What were they talking about? Her work. Right.

"Cool," she repeated. "That's me."

Not quite.

At this moment, she was unbelievably not cool. She felt off balance, not sure how to navigate this new water when she'd vowed to keep an ocean between her and the man standing across the room.

"You've taken Dad's practice to the next level," she said, groping for a topic that wasn't so personal to her. As soon as the words were out, she realized her father's legacy made it worse.

"I'm still grateful for the opportunity your father gave me," Ethan answered, his voice so solemn it made her throat ache. "His reputation is the backbone of the clinic."

This wasn't right either. His words were too serious in the quiet intimacy of the kitchen. Lainey didn't do intimacy anymore. If the past had taught her one thing, it was not to let emotional connections influence her life. That only ended in pain for everyone involved.

She cocked her head to one side, hoping to lighten the mood. "When did you become such a Boy Scout? What happened to badass Ethan Daniels?"

His back stiffened, his molten eyes going icy. "In case you've forgotten, me being a badass tore your family apart. I changed a lot after you left. I changed fast."

"I haven't forgotten anything," she whispered. "What happened wasn't your fault." She didn't realize how much she needed to say those words until they were out.

She'd come to see her miscarriage and the complications that resulted in her infertility as a sign that she was never meant to be a mother. A punishment for reaching for something she couldn't have. The blame sat squarely on her shoulders. She suddenly needed Ethan to understand that. "I was the one—"

"Don't go there." His hand chopped through the air. "I didn't come here to rehash ancient history."

"So why *are* you here?"

The ten-million-dollar question, Ethan thought. He'd been surprised to run into her, but what shocked him more was how quickly his initial anger had disappeared. Because Lainey looked as miserable as he'd felt for so long, and despite how she'd hurt him, he didn't think she deserved that.

He forced himself to remember how she'd run off when he'd put himself on the line for her. He'd had way too much experience with being deserted by the women he loved and had learned the hard way that he couldn't rely on anyone else. He needed to keep his distance from her.

"I'm here for Vera." Best to leave the past where it belonged. For everyone involved.

"Okay." She gave him a tentative smile. The hair on the back of his neck stood on end.

He forced himself to look away, glancing out the window where night had fallen in earnest. The kitchen glowed in comparison, creating a strange yet familiar sense of closeness between them.

Ethan cleared his throat. "I care…" he began but lost his train of thought for a moment as he watched her chest rise when she sucked in a deep breath.

"About?" she prompted, her green eyes turning dark.

"I care…about your mom," he finished, keeping emotion

out of his voice. "We've worked together for a long time. She and your dad were more a family to me than my own crazy father. Vera has always supported me. We're friends, and I hate to see her in the hospital. It's not right."

Lainey jerked her head in agreement but didn't speak so he continued. "I'll do whatever I can to help her. The clinic has a big stake in the adoption fair."

He paused, wondering if his convoluted thoughts made more sense spoken out loud. "This will be easier if things aren't messed up between us. The way I see it, stuff happened. We were kids. It doesn't matter now."

"It doesn't matter," she repeated, as if absorbing each word.

He nodded. "Water under the bridge."

"Yesterday's news," she countered.

He thought about that one for a moment. The glint in her eye told him he was on shaky ground. "Or maybe not."

She pushed herself away from the counter. "You should go now, Ethan."

He took a step closer. "If you need me to..."

"I don't," she said, almost yelling as she backed into the kitchen sink. She closed her eyes for a moment. When she spoke again, her voice was calm, her gaze emotionless. "I don't need anything from you."

Her words poured over his head like a bucket of cold water. He turned away. "I guess some things never change," he called over his shoulder, "because the way I remember it, you never did."

He slammed the door behind him and stalked down the stairs, pausing at the bottom when he heard something clatter against the kitchen wall.

He wanted to charge back up the steps but knew whatever had smashed into the wall had clearly been meant for his head.

She didn't need him, he repeated. How long would it take before he'd finally be clear on that? Ten years ago, he'd offered her everything he had: his heart, his name, the rest of his life. She'd thrown it all back in his face, walked away without even a goodbye.

He headed across the driveway to his truck. Vera told him the universe makes you repeat your mistakes until you get them right. If that was the case, this summer was bound to be the biggest lesson of his life.

Chapter Three

Lainey rapped her fist against the door a second time. "Come on. I know you're in there." She glanced at the Land Cruiser, running her fingers through her tangled mess of hair. Her mother had told her Ethan was staying at the clinic, and she didn't know where else to go.

She turned back when the door opened. Ethan stood in the doorway, the house dark behind him. He wore a pair of faded cargo shorts and nothing else. She blinked, momentarily distracted by his bare chest and the muscles corded along his stomach, disappearing beneath the waistband of his shorts.

If there'd been any doubt, she now knew for certain the boy she remembered was long gone. From the shadow of stubble that covered his jaw to the powerful arms, Ethan's body was one hundred percent man.

He squinted against the morning light peeking through the surrounding trees. "Lainey?" His voice was rough with sleep.

"I need you," she began then realized how stupid she sounded after last night.

A look of disbelief flashed in his eyes before his gaze darkened. "That was quick." He leaned against the doorjamb. "I get it because you're only human and all. But there is no way—"

"Not like that. It's Pita."

He straightened. "What happened?" he asked, all business.

"She didn't eat last night or this morning—" Lainey worked to keep the panic out of her voice. "She threw up then had an accident in the middle of the night. There was blood in it…more this morning." Tears clogged her throat. "She's bleeding, Ethan."

He wrapped his big hands around hers, using his thumbs to pry apart her clenched fists and rub her palms. "It's okay," he said, his gaze never leaving her face. "I'll take a look at her."

"I don't know anything about her, her history or age. I don't even know if she's been fixed." Her voice trembled and he squeezed her hands harder. "She isn't really mine…"

She knew she was overreacting but couldn't stop it. She'd compartmentalized her own pain, avoided any connections that might lead to more hurt all the while telling herself she was okay. The past was in the past. But she wasn't healed emotionally and her irrational fear over the dog made her wonder if she ever would be. "What if she's pregnant and…" Her voice trailed off. "There's a lot of blood."

He drew her into a tight hug. "We'll take care of her."

Lainey wanted to pull away but pressed her cheek into the crook of his neck. His skin was warm, and the hair on his chest tickled her face. He smelled like sleep, soap and the spicy male scent that was intrinsically him—a scent that hadn't changed in ten years.

He kept his hands on her, running his palms along her bare arms, looking deep into her eyes. "Are you okay?"

Lainey wiped the back of her hand across her nose and nodded. "I'm fine," she said around a hiccup.

"Uh-huh." He cocked his head to one side and studied her.

"Really, I am." She didn't want this. Hated feeling so exposed, like he could see into the depths of her soul.

He looked unconvinced. "Let's get to it then."

It wasn't even 7:00 a.m., but Lainey guessed the temperature had already climbed past eighty degrees. Still her skin felt impossibly cold when he let her go. He disappeared into the house for a moment then stepped back onto the porch in a wrinkled polo shirt.

She led him around the SUV. The hatch was already open. The dog lay on a makeshift bed of blankets Lainey had piled into the cargo area.

"Hey there," Ethan cooed. Pita lifted her head in response. Her tail thumped once, but she didn't jump up. After a moment she pressed her face into the towel and whined.

"Hold her still."

Lainey positioned her hands on the side of the dog's head. Pita yelped when Ethan pushed his fingers into her belly. Her large brown eyes found Lainey's.

"It's all right," Lainey whispered. "You are going to be just fine, my sweet pain in the ass."

Ethan's hands paused.

"Pita." She huffed out a breath. "Pain in the ass."

One side of his mouth kicked up as he moved his fingers along the dog's abdomen. "Cute."

Lainey couldn't pin her hopes on this man. His rejection ten years ago had burned so badly she'd sworn never to give herself like that again to anyone. She'd spent a long time getting Ethan out of her system, remaking herself from the lovestruck girl who'd literally fallen at his feet to an independent woman who didn't need anyone—any man—to rescue her.

"What's going on with her? Will she…"

"I need to take X-rays. It feels like there's a blockage. Probably something she ate."

Lainey's fingers flew to her mouth. "Oh, no. The hamburger." She bent forward to kiss the dog's head. "I'm so sorry."

"It wasn't the hamburger." He leveled a serious look at her. "This isn't your fault. Animals eat things they shouldn't. Keeps me in business most weeks. With any luck she'll be back to normal in a day or so."

"So she's not…"

"She's not pregnant, Lainey."

Relief mixed with a fleeting sense of disappointment welled inside her. She tried to keep her expression neutral, but Ethan must have read something because his eyes narrowed and he turned away.

"I'm going to move her to the clinic. Steph comes in at seven. She can help."

"Stephanie Rand?"

"She's my tech," he answered with a nod. "You two hung out in high school, right?"

Lainey swallowed. "Best friends since second grade."

He scooped Pita into his arms. "Let's go then." He strode across the dirt path that led to the main clinic building, carrying Pita like he was cradling a baby.

Lainey stood alone next to the Land Cruiser. Stephanie Rand was another person Lainey hadn't spoken to since she'd hightailed it out of Brevia—one of the few people who knew the full extent of what had happened to Lainey ten years ago. She'd wanted Lainey to tell Ethan everything right away— her parents, too. But Lainey couldn't admit how badly she'd failed them all.

Maybe that was why Lainey had cut ties with Steph when she'd left, hadn't returned her friend's calls or answered emails. Any reminder of the past hurt too much.

Ethan's voice brought her back to the present. "Are you coming?" He waited at the back door of the clinic.

She reached up and slammed shut the SUV's rear hatch. "Yes," she called, and he disappeared inside the building.

Lainey's footsteps crunched on the gravel driveway. She looked around the property that had once belonged to her father's family. The clinic stood where it always had, tucked into a far corner of the lot in a converted farmhouse where her dad had grown up.

To the left stood the original barn that housed any large breed animals under the clinic's care and the All Creatures Great & Small Animal Shelter her mother had founded after her father died.

Guilt stabbed at her chest, the same guilt she always felt when she thought of her dad. She'd been on assignment in a remote section of India when he'd died. She'd missed her chance to say goodbye, lost the opportunity to reconcile with him.

When she'd phoned her mother two days later from Bangladesh, Vera had told her she wasn't needed. "Ethan and Julia are taking care of things" had been her mother's exact words. Lainey had drowned her grief in a bottle of cheap wine, blamed the dull ache in her head on a hangover and flown to Nairobi for a shoot covering that country's dwindling elephant population.

She'd done what she did best: run away from her pain and try to convince herself she was living her perfect life.

Right now her feet itched to scurry to the Land Cruiser. But not even a soul-crushing fear was strong enough to make her desert the dog. She would not inflict the pain of abandonment on another living being, even one of the four-legged variety.

She followed Ethan through the back door of the animal hospital and found him bent over Pita in one of the exam rooms. Lainey crouched near Pita's face. "I'm right here, girl."

Ethan straightened. "Steph's getting the X-ray equipment warmed up. We need to figure out what's causing the blockage. Surgery's an option but a lot riskier. It would be easier if she could get it out on her own."

"She poops like a goose," Lainey murmured to herself.

"Hopefully," Ethan said with a short laugh, "that will work in her favor."

Lainey was too worried to be embarrassed by discussing her dog's potty habits with her ex-fiancé.

Ethan lifted Pita again. "I'll have her back to you in a few minutes."

Lainey sank into the mud-colored vinyl chair that sat against one wall. She closed her eyes but refused to pray. There was a time when she'd spent days on end praying, holed up in her bedroom, her knees hugged in a fetal position. She'd offered prayers, promises, threats—anything so she wouldn't lose the life growing inside her.

In the end, nothing had worked. Lainey had given up on prayer just like everything else.

The door creaked open. She stood, expecting Ethan and Pita. Stephanie Rand stepped into the room. "He'll be a few minutes more," she said. "I wanted to say hi."

"Hey, Steph." Lainey wondered for a moment if she would have recognized her old friend if she passed her on the street. "You look great."

The other woman gave a bark of laughter and finger combed her high bangs. "You always were a bad liar, Lainey." Steph smoothed a hand across the front of her purple scrubs. "I still have twenty pounds to go on my baby weight."

"You have a baby?"

"Three boys. Although Joe Jr.'s eight and the twins turned six last month."

Lainey's eyes widened. "You married Joe Wilkens?" she

asked, picturing Steph's high school boyfriend. "Your last name…"

"He's my ex."

"Sorry."

Stephanie smiled. "There you go again. You told me Joe was a no-good loser thirteen years ago. He split when the twins were eight months."

"That's awful."

"He was a terrible daddy and a worse husband." She flashed a rueful smile. "Too bad I never lost the hots for him. He looked at me and I got pregnant." She slapped her hand against her mouth. "I'm sorry. I didn't mean…"

"It's okay," Lainey said, surprised to find she meant it. She took a deep breath and said, "I've missed you, Steph." She meant that, too, although she hadn't realized it.

Tension seemed to ease from Steph's shoulders. Her smile turned watery. "Me, too."

"Maybe I could meet your boys sometime."

"They'll have you wrapped around their grubby fingers in five seconds flat," Ethan commented as he walked through the open door. He'd changed into a pair of khaki pants and a navy polo shirt with the clinic's name sewn above the pocket.

Stephanie gave him a playful slap on the shoulder. "Not everyone's as big a sucker as Uncle Ethan."

Uncle Ethan. He'd always loved kids, wanted enough for a football team he'd joked with her.

Wanted to try again.

Another layer of the pain she'd buried uncurled in her stomach.

"Lainey?"

She looked up. Ethan and Steph stared at her. "Where's Pita?" she asked.

Ethan's brows furrowed. "I just said she's asleep in one of the kennels. She was a trooper for the X-rays."

"Right." She tucked a loose strand of hair behind her ear. "What did you find?"

He flipped a switch on the metal box hanging on the wall and it lit with an iridescent glow. "There's definitely something in there." He slid the X-ray into place. "I'm not sure… uh…what exactly…"

The two women stepped closer to the bright light.

"Oh, no…" Lainey gasped. She recognized the scalloped edges that were white within the dark area that must have been Pita's stomach.

Steph whistled under her breath. "Wowee, Lain, I wouldn't have pegged you for a thong girl."

Within seconds Lainey's cheeks were as hot as asphalt in the middle of August. "There's no way…" She leaned in inches from the machine. "You can't tell that's a thong."

"Lots of dogs are partial to skivvies." Steph traced the tip of one short nail along the X-ray. "But even twisted like that, there's not enough fabric for regular undies. The question is who are you shopping at Victoria's Secret to impress?"

"Steph!" Lainey and Ethan shouted at once.

Embarrassed beyond belief, Lainey made herself focus on Pita. She hitched her chin and turned to Ethan. "The question is can you get them out? I'm not sure I could take it if this killed her."

"Kinky," Steph muttered.

"Stephanie!" Lainey and Ethan yelled again.

"I'm going to check on the patient," Steph said.

"Good idea." Ethan ran his hands through his hair. "You've got about fifteen minutes until your first appointment."

Ethan nodded and closed the door. He turned to Lainey, trying hard not to think about the unmistakable lace shining in the light of the X-ray machine. "I'm going to give her something that will soften her digestive track, move the object through."

He prided himself on his emotional detachment from his patients, convinced the distance made him a more effective doctor. Maybe it was the fact that he'd gone without his morning caffeine fix. Or his body's haywire reaction to Lainey. He felt punch-drunk with relief that her dog had a good chance at recovering.

"Can I take her home?"

"She needs to stay where we can monitor her. If there's no progress by tonight, I'll schedule her for surgery in the morning."

Her eyes widened. "Surgery?"

"She can't keep your panties...the obstruction needs to come out. It's too dangerous otherwise."

She nodded but looked down.

His insides coiled with frustration. He'd seen too much pain in her eyes—been the cause of most of it—to take any more. As much as he wanted to hate her, he couldn't turn her away.

Steph opened the door. "Edith McIntire and Bubbles are waiting in Exam Two."

Damn. "I'm coming."

"Can I see her?" Lainey's voice was barely a whisper.

"Of course. Leave your number with the front desk. I'll call if anything changes." He forced himself to turn away. "Steph, would you take her to the back?"

"You bet."

As she moved past him, he grabbed Lainey's arm. "I'll take care of her."

Her chin bobbed.

"She's going to be okay," he assured her. "I promise."

She sucked in a breath and recoiled as if he'd slapped her. He realized his mistake, but it was too late to take back the words. The same words he'd whispered to her in a hospital ten summers ago.

Her eyes searched his. "You should have learned by now." Her tone held no reproach, only sadness. "You shouldn't make promises you don't have the power to keep."

She walked out, but her voice pounded like a sledgehammer inside his head. He'd promised her the baby—his child—would be fine. But nothing had gone right that summer. She'd lost the baby, he'd lost her and neither of them had ever been the same.

It took several minutes for his mind to clear enough to officially begin his morning. Even a full load of patients couldn't stop thoughts of Lainey from consuming him. Her stiff shoulders and guarded expression, the sadness in her eyes.

Lainey had left him high and dry, and part of him wanted her punished for it, but he'd also shared in the blame. He'd known about her crush on him and should have never gotten involved with her in the first place. He could have spared them both a world of heartache by just leaving her alone.

The breakup with Julia had been a blow, more to his ego than his heart. They'd outgrown each other long before she'd dumped him. Still, his emotions had become numb, and being with Lainey made him feel so alive. Maybe he should have given her more, told her that he was falling in love with her, but every time he needed someone he ended up hurt.

His own mother had abandoned him and his dad when Ethan was just a kid. He remembered sitting on the bed as she packed her overstuffed suitcase. She'd told him it was better for all of them, but Ethan's father had made it very clear that the blame lay completely on Ethan's narrow shoulders.

He'd been shy, always staying close to his mom, who was the one person who made him feel safe. His boyish need had become too much for his free-spirited mother, his dad told him. She couldn't handle being shackled in that way.

He figured that was why his relationship with Lainey had been so mind-blowing—he'd needed her with an intensity he hadn't felt for years. And despite his trying to hide it, she'd felt it, and the weight of his love proved too much yet again.

He couldn't rewrite the past, but if he could put aside his own pain and resentment and keep his need for her out of the equation—even for a few short weeks—he might have the chance to make amends for shattering both their lives.

Once and for all.

Downtown Brevia looked much the same as Lainey remembered. Redbrick buildings and Victorian-type storefronts with colorful awnings lined the main street. Instead of the pharmacy and family-owned furniture stores she knew growing up, signs for boutique-type clothing and craft retailers welcomed the overflow of tourists from the Smoky Mountains and nearby Asheville.

She wondered absently how many of these new merchants were locals or whether some of them were recent transplants to the small southern town. Hoping for the latter, she reached for the door of the local newspaper, *The Brevia Times*. Vera had wanted her to meet the reporter who'd been the media contact for previous adoption fairs, and as nervous as Lainey was about facing anyone in Brevia, she needed to keep herself occupied and her mind off Pita.

To her surprise, the man who leaned against the desk in the lobby was a familiar face. "Tim?" she asked with pleasure. "I didn't know you worked here."

"Hey there." Tim Reynolds, one of her closest high school friends, stepped forward to hug her. He looked a lot like he had back then, shaggy blond hair and small wire-rimmed glasses. Smart and serious, that was Tim. "I'm the editor of this little paper now. I heard you were coming in today and wanted to make sure you got a warm welcome."

Lainey released a nervous breath. "I thought you were in Atlanta."

He shrugged. "Brevia may not be much of a news hotbed, but it's hard to stay away."

"Tell me about it," Lainey agreed with a sharp laugh.

He didn't let go of her arms. "How are you?"

She tried to shrug out of his grasp, pulling back sharply when he didn't release her right away. "Okay, I guess."

He adjusted his belt over the stomach that was a little large for his slight frame. "It's so good you're back."

"I'm still shocked to be here, but it's only for the summer." She thought about Pita but decided against mentioning her worry over the dog. Tim knew Ethan well—they'd gone to the same university, and although Tim was Lainey's age, his older brother had been Ethan's best friend growing up.

Tim had been at the church on her wedding day. He'd been the one to find Lainey shaking uncontrollably at the back of the sanctuary as she went to leave Ethan the note explaining her decision to leave. Tim hadn't seemed shocked and hadn't tried to argue with her. He'd simply taken the letter with a promise to deliver it and assurance that everything would be all right.

He'd been wrong, but Lainey was still grateful for his unconditional support. Now she appreciated that although he'd been a friend of Ethan's, she saw no judgment in his gaze.

"If you need anything while you're in town, just let me know." He stared at her so intently, Lainey had to look away. "In fact, I'm going to take over coverage of the adoption fair this year."

"Are you sure?" Lainey figured that should make her happy, but instead her stomach flipped uneasily. "Don't you have more important things to do?"

"Nothing is more important than you," he answered.

"Oh." Lainey gave herself a mental shake. She'd been worried about the anger she'd encounter but now was uncomfortable at Tim's friendliness. "I mean, thank you." She took a small step back and patted her large tote. "I brought this year's press kit. Should we take a look?"

He studied her another long moment then nodded. "We'll make a great team, Lainey," he said, gesturing down a long hall. "This way to my office."

Chapter Four

"You wear a thong? Really?"

Lainey leveled a look at her sister. "One—why is that so hard to believe? And two—it's not really the point of the story."

"I know, I know." Julia held up her hands. "I just figured you more the granny panty type."

Lainey didn't answer, unwilling to own up to how right Julia was. About ninety-five percent of the items in her lingerie drawer—if you could call it that—were of the basic cotton variety. Her work schedule didn't leave time for dating. At least that's what she told herself. It was easier than admitting the truth.

She'd dated a few guys casually between assignments in her early twenties. But something had changed. As her friends had begun to marry and start families, she'd drifted away from them.

Her biological clock should have stopped ticking since

she couldn't have children. Since that hadn't happened, she'd taken far-flung assignments, spending more time on the road. It had been great for her career and much easier than watching the people around her build lives she could never have.

Her gaze settled on Julia's round belly. "So where is Jeff?" she asked, changing the subject away from her underpants. It was odd to see Julia back in their hometown but stranger still that she was so pregnant and here alone.

With some effort, Julia hoisted herself out of the chair and paced the length of their mother's small hospital room.

Vera had been taken to one of several daily physical therapy appointments. The doctor would come in after this latest round to discuss her rehabilitation in more detail.

"He's in South America," Julia finally answered. She stood at the window looking out at the hospital's courtyard, her long fingers massaging either side of her lower back. "He had research to do, and we didn't think it was good to spend the whole pregnancy in the mountains of Brazil. He'll be back before my due date."

"But you won't want to settle in Brevia with Jeff's job at the university. Why aren't you at Mom's? Is it because I was coming home?"

Julia shook her head. "I needed my own space. Mom gets a little overbearing, you know? I'm renting an apartment near downtown. Just temporary, of course."

"That makes sense," Lainey agreed, although something in Julia's tone made her wonder if she was getting the whole story.

"There was nothing keeping me in Columbus with him gone," Julia continued. "I can cut hair anywhere."

"You still work? I thought—"

"A couple hours a week. My blood pressure skyrockets if I stand any longer. Val says I can come back after the baby's born." Julia shrugged. "But who knows where Jeff and I will be by then."

Lainey's mouth dropped open. She clamped it shut before Julia turned around. "You're working at The Hair House?"

Julia glanced over her shoulder and smiled. "It's almost as hard to believe as you in a thong."

"I didn't mean…" Lainey's voice trailed off. Val Dupree had owned "The Best Little Hair House in Brevia" since they were kids. She couldn't picture Julia at Val's any more than she could see her sister in Brevia for the long haul.

She took a deep breath. Julia had only been in New York six months before returning to Brevia that summer. She'd wanted Ethan back, but Lainey had already been pregnant. Julia was so angry she'd left town again as soon as Ethan had offered to marry Lainey.

Lainey didn't know if she had the power to fix all the broken pieces in her relationship with her sister. Since she was here for the better part of the summer, she'd give it her best shot. "Val probably realized how lucky she is to have you," she offered, although it sounded weak to her ears.

"Why?" Julia countered. "Because most of her girls think Marie Osmond is the epitome of high style?"

"Among other reasons."

Julia walked to the chair. "Don't blow sunshine," she said with an eye roll. "You got out and I was sucked back in. Mom's already given me the 'you should have stayed in college' lecture. I messed up. Bad."

The ability to disappoint Vera—at least they now had that in common. Lainey felt a twinge of sympathy, an emotion she'd never associated with Julia. "You had some decent modeling jobs at first. Maybe if you'd had more time…"

"Being voted 'prettiest girl' in your country-bumpkin senior class doesn't count in New York."

Lainey shrugged. "All the 'nicest girl' award got me was

the assumption that I'd say yes to anyone who wanted to cheat off me. I should've been voted class doormat. I was always jealous of you in high school. You were popular, prom queen and had the football captain for your boyfriend."

"Until my little sister stole him away. Nice girl. Yeah, right." Julia laughed, but there was no humor in it. "I wish the voters could've seen that move."

"You'd broken up with him," Lainey said through clenched teeth, bristling at the decade-old accusation. Guilt was one thing, but Lainey only let things go as far as they had with Ethan because she thought Julia had moved on.

"We were on a break," Julia fired back.

"Give *me* a break. You ditched him for the big-city modeling agent. Chewed up his heart, spit it out then ground your heel in it for good measure." The idea that Lainey could have stolen Ethan from her sister was ridiculous. "I was there, remember?"

Julia leaned forward. "I remember. And you're right. Ethan and I were over long before you were in the picture. Still, you did the chewing, spitting and grinding."

"No," Lainey whispered, finally ready to admit the truth. "That was my problem. After you left there wasn't enough of his heart for me to hold on to."

Julia inhaled sharply. "Are you joking?" she began. "Do you know how long he waited—"

The door banged open, interrupting her. Vera's wheelchair rolled into the room, pushed by a strapping physical therapist who looked like he'd just left a biker bar. His bald head glimmered in the fluorescent light, the lines around his eyes etched deep as a dried riverbed as he watched Vera, his gaze filled with rapt adoration.

Even pushing sixty and ravaged by the stroke, Vera radiated energy like light from the mother ship to the opposite sex.

Vera glanced between Lainey and Julia. "Can hear you down hall." She spoke slowly to make her pronunciation clear.

"Sorry, Mom," both women chorused.

"Fighting no good. I need you to help." She took a breath, but the next words she spoke were so garbled Lainey couldn't understand them.

"Don't push yourself," the physical therapist said as he helped Vera back into bed.

He turned, flexing a skull tattoo in Lainey's direction. "Your mom made good progress this morning. Her left leg is about seventy-five percent of its normal strength."

"Stupid right leg," Vera mumbled.

"It'll come," the burly man said with surprising softness as he tucked a quilt around her. "Rest now. You earned it."

Vera smiled at him and Lainey saw color creep up his neck. Her mother could wrap any man around her finger.

Lainey noticed a bright sheen of perspiration across her mother's forehead. Vera used every ounce of strength to get better while Lainey bickered with Julia over ancient history. She was here to help, Lainey reminded herself, not stumble down the rocky path to bad memory lane.

She stepped closer and lifted Vera's fingers. She looked at Julia. "I guess we should stick to discussing the adoption event," she whispered.

"And current local gossip," Julia added. "The kind that doesn't involve our family."

Lainey choked out a laugh at that.

Vera squeezed Lainey's hand. Her eyes fluttered open. "More like it," she said and snuggled deeper against the pillows.

Lainey smiled, impressed but not surprised that even in her condition, Vera Morgan could bend her daughters to her will with a few chosen words. She'd honed that skill for years.

"Heard about your dog?" Vera asked, her eyes concerned.

"Nothing yet."

"Ethan is best. He'll do good."

Lainey nodded. She thought about the care Ethan had given Pita and the tenderness he'd shown to her. A slow ache built in her heart. "I stopped by the shelter office after I left the clinic." She needed to regain control.

"You get the box?"

Lainey pointed to a large plastic storage tub in the corner of the room. "Rest for a bit, Mom. Then we'll go through it."

Julia patted Vera's leg. "I need to go."

Vera's left hand clamped around Julia's wrist. "You stay."

Her tone brooked no argument, although Julia gave it her best shot.

"I need to check in with Val, see if I can pick up some hours if my doctor approves."

Vera's hold didn't loosen. "Later."

"Fine." Vera let go of Julia's hand as she stood. "I need to pee first. It feels like this kid has his heel shoved against my bladder."

Lainey blew out a short breath as Julia closed the bathroom door. She felt her mother's eyes on her. "This doesn't change anything."

"You good girl," Vera said, reaching out to her.

Lainey pushed up from the bed. "I don't know what you expect, but me being here isn't going to make the past go away. I can do my penance this summer, but I can't change what happened. What I did." She couldn't change who she was, how the tragedy had changed her. Forever.

"Good girl," Vera repeated.

Her mother used the same tone Lainey did with Pita. She didn't know whether to laugh or cry. She tucked her hair behind her ear. "We'll go through the plans while you rest," she said, but her mother's eyes had already slipped closed.

Lainey smoothed the quilt again and turned for the big box in the corner.

Work on the adoption event kept Lainey occupied the rest of the day. Julia had stayed at the hospital until lunchtime, the two sisters careful not to let the topic stray from animals needing a home.

The call came in around four o'clock. Her hands shook as she stared at the clinic's number on her cell phone.

"Answer it," her mother said.

She brought the phone to her ear, expecting Ethan's voice.

"Lainey?" Stephanie Rand said. "She's okay."

A strangled sob escaped her lips. "Oh, thank God."

Steph continued, "I don't think you want your undies back, but at least they're out."

"Can I come get her?" Lainey spoke around the lump of tears knotting at the back of her throat.

"We'd like to keep her overnight, just to make sure she's back to normal. You can pick her up first thing in the morning."

Lainey made a squeaky sound she hoped passed for a 'yes' and hung up.

She looked at her mother. The deep understanding in Vera's gaze almost sent her over the edge.

"Underpants," she mumbled, her voice wobbly. "How dumb." Stupid to make everything so personal.

"Go home."

"I'm fine."

"Home," her mother said again, pointing at the door.

Lainey knew she should argue, insist on staying, but fatigue settled over her. She leaned in and kissed her mother's cheek. "I'll be back in the morning." She traced the corner of Vera's lopsided mouth.

"Bring polish."

"What?"

Vera wiggled her fingers in the air. "Upstairs bathroom, bottom drawer. Pink polish, 'Touch of Love.'"

Despite her jumbled emotions, Lainey smiled. "We'll have a mini spa day."

Vera fingered Lainey's hair. "Julia can cut for you."

"I like my hair, Mom." She covered her mother's hand with hers and pulled it away, straightening from the bed.

"Too long. Julia helps."

Her back stiffened. "I'll see you tomorrow," she said quickly and turned for the door. Vera never approved of her hair, her clothes, her makeup—or lack thereof.

Why should it be different now?

Her mother had only one definition of beautiful: blond hair, blue-eyed with a Barbie's unrealistic measurements. Vera had epitomized the look in her day, and Julia was the spitting image of their mother.

Lainey was a chip off the Eastern European block of her father's family with her unruly hair and olive skin. At least she'd gotten her mother's button nose, although it looked out of place set between her almond-shaped eyes and too-wide mouth.

She eyed the hospital exit sign like it was the finish line of the Boston Marathon. When the automatic doors slid open, a wave of aggressively humid air hit her square in the face and she slowed. Everything moved at a snail's pace during a Brevia summer.

"No," she told herself as she unlocked the Land Cruiser and slid behind the steering wheel. She took a few deep breaths and pulled out of the parking lot, determined to hold herself in check.

The heat did not own her.

This town would not bully her.

Her mother could not control her any more.

She forced herself on a four-mile run when she got back

to the house. Better to sweat out her emotions than indulge in another pint of Chubby Hubby.

After a long, cool shower, she slipped into a pair of cotton shorts and a black tank top. She'd spent the previous night awake with Pita, so she now began unpacking her clothes into the same dresser that had once held sets of Garanimals outfits. The shadow of the bed's ruffled canopy fell over her like a weight.

The walls seemed to hum with long-ago conversations and emotions. She couldn't watch television without imagining her father asleep in his faded leather recliner and didn't want to soak in the tub that held the smell of her mother's perfume.

She finally got in her car and drove until she saw the lights of Piggly Wiggly. She didn't need groceries but flipped through magazines, studying the layouts and lighting of the photos, until she felt sleepy.

She bought *Cosmopolitan*, *In Style* and a box of dog biscuits. As she put the bag into the cargo area, something cold and wet nudged her thigh. She spun around.

"Pita." Lainey's heart thudded against her rib cage. She dropped to her knees. "Oh, sweetie. How are you? How did you get here?"

Glancing up, she had a brief glimpse of a dark head before Pita's front paws slammed into her chest. She went over backward in a tangle of arms, legs and dog limbs.

"Easy, girl." Ethan's deep voice cut through the quiet. He grabbed Pita's collar and hauled the dog off her.

Lainey lay flat on her back, legs splayed across the asphalt. Ethan loomed over her, fingers curled around the dog's collar. Under the bright parking lot light, one corner of his mouth kicked up and his eyes danced, sending sparks flying in their deep centers.

"I guess she's better," Lainey managed to say, wheezing a

little as she tried to gather her wits. At least she had the good sense to close her legs.

"Yep," was his only answer.

"How did you find me?"

He shrugged. "I didn't think you'd want to wait until morning, so I was driving out to Vera's when I saw your car. Not a lot of fancy SUVs in Brevia."

She lifted a hand into the air. "You want to help me up?"

He cocked his head to one side. "I kind of like you down there. I imagine you groveling for forgiveness at my feet."

"Fine," she mumbled and looked away. She started to drop her arm, but he released his hold on the dog and grabbed her wrist. He hauled her to her feet so fast she stumbled forward into him. It was like falling against the side of a mountain.

She pushed out her breath, not wanting to inhale his scent, and tried to step away. He held her close.

"I fixed your dog," he said, his voice rough against her ear. "I guess you owe me an apology *and* a thank you. How do you want to settle your debt?"

A hundred wicked images flashed across her mind in the space of a second. A shiver of anticipation traveled the length of her body, starting at the top of her head and leaving a trail of goose bumps from the base of her neck to the tips of her toes. She shoved away from him and crossed her arms over her chest, suddenly aware that she wasn't wearing a bra.

His eyes gleamed black as night as he stared at her shirt.

She dug in her heels and blurted, "I already apologized. I left you the letter. Right after…" Her voice faded as a murderous expression crossed his face. "I thought you would…"

"I burned it."

The words slammed into her with the force of a hurricane. "Did you even read it?"

He looked away for a few beats then jerked his head. "Before I burned it."

Her eyes widened. She'd poured her soul cnto those pages, hoping he'd come after her. She'd spent days in that hotel room in Charlotte waiting for him, wanting to start over and make a life together. Hope had faded into uncertainty and finally a despair that had left her curled on the floor of the hotel bathroom, the blood vessels in her eyes broken from crying so hard.

"Do you know what it took for me to tell you those things? You never…"

"Do you know what it took," he shot back, "for me to stand at the front of that church waiting for you? Half the town watched me get dumped on my wedding day."

Her anger melted away as fresh waves of guilt washed over her, filling her lungs until her entire body ached with it. "I didn't dump you," she whispered.

"Pardon me if I don't get the terminology right. What would you call it? Jilted? Screwed over? Left behind?"

Is that what he thought? That by leaving she'd abandoned him? Maybe he couldn't understand how it had hurt her to watch the pity in his eyes as he'd said he'd still marry her. She'd been so grief-stricken and ashamed, she couldn't face him and the letter had seemed her only option.

If he'd burned the letter after what she'd written, she knew without a doubt she'd done the right thing. All these years later there was no comfort in that fact.

"Things happen for a reason," she said, not believing it. Acid rose in her gut as she forced a smile. "The way I see it now, you should have been relieved. Didn't I let you off the biggest hook in history?"

Chapter Five

She had him there, Ethan thought.

Those were the exact words his buddies used when they'd taken him out to the local bar to get hammered after finding the ring and the note on the bathroom sink in the basement of the church that day.

Ethan, drunk off his gourd and egged on by a friend, had burned it in a bonfire out at Stroud's Run Lake. He'd cursed himself and his wicked hangover the next morning when he'd wanted to read her words again. He wasn't about to admit that now.

"You're right," he told her. "I just wish you'd figured it out before I put on the monkey suit."

"I wish a lot of things, Ethan."

The mix of sympathy and sadness in her eyes grabbed at his gut. He didn't want her sympathy. "You did us both a favor, I guess. I was a lousy boyfriend and would've made a worse husband."

"Did you ever come close again?" she asked, then covered her mouth as if she couldn't believe she'd spoken the words. "I'm sorry. It's none of my business."

He managed a smile. "I escaped the hangman's noose once," he said, drawing out his vowels to sound like a typical good ole boy. "It won't catch me again."

"Oh."

Pain flashed in her eyes. He told himself it was better than sympathy. "How about you? Anything serious?"

She blinked several times then shook her head. "I'm away so much for work. It doesn't leave time for a social life."

"You like all the travel?"

The dog jumped into the back of the SUV, and she patted its head, not making eye contact with him. "It's part of the job. Why?"

"I'd always pegged you for the homemaker type. You know, a couple of kids, carpool, cookies baking in the oven— the whole bit."

"Shows how well you knew me."

"Ain't that the truth."

His gaze fell to where her hand rested on Pita, her fingers trembling. Something inside him stilled. Despite his anger, he wanted to reach out, wipe away the sorrow neither of them could leave behind.

Their eyes met and she snatched her hand away. "I should go."

"How's your mama?" he asked, suddenly not wanting to leave her.

She sighed. "We met with the doctor earlier. She's improving, but it's slow. Her speech is better. Hopefully, she'll come home in the next couple of weeks—once her right side improves. She has a lot of therapy in front of her."

"How's she dealing with everything?"

"She's demanding, prickly, hot-tempered and charming the daylights out of everyone at the hospital."

"Typical Vera."

"Exactly."

"It's not the same at the shelter without her."

One side of Lainey's mouth curved. "Nothing ever is."

Darkness descended over the parking lot. A quarter moon shone overhead and a streetlight glowed a lane over. Shadows covered Lainey's face so he couldn't read her expression.

"Call me if anything changes with Pita."

"Thank you. For everything."

He stepped back as she reached up and pulled the hatch down.

"Sure," he said at the same time the door's edge smashed into her head.

Muttering a curse, Lainey pressed her hands to her head. Pita immediately stood, barked once and pushed against Lainey's shoulder, her tail wagging hard.

She sucked in shallow breaths. Ethan pulled her near as he sat on the raised bumper. "Let me take a look." He pried her fingers away. "How bad is it?"

"Not awful, but I might throw up." She laughed but he heard tears in her voice. "You may not want to be so close."

He didn't get up and she didn't move. "Pita, down."

"How did you do that?" she asked as Pita plopped on her belly.

He clicked on the dim light above the cargo space and tilted her head toward it. "Your mom taught me."

"Figures."

"There's a little blood. Do you have a towel?"

She raised her hands into the light. The tips of her fingers showed traces of red. "Maybe some napkins up front."

"Do *not* try to stand."

"It's really not serious," she said softly. "Feels like slamming a door shut on your fingers." But she stayed put on the bumper.

His gaze flicked to the dog. "You. Stay."

He rummaged through the front seat and found a stack of Dunkin' Donuts napkins and a package of wet wipes under a large camera bag.

When he came back around the SUV, Lainey had covered her eyes with the heels of her hands. He tugged on her outstretched fingers until she raised her head.

"This may sting."

"I saw stars for a minute. I doubt—ouch! Hey…"

He dabbed a wet wipe at the scrape. "I told you." He spread her hair so he could have a closer look. He almost didn't notice how silky the strands were as they slipped through his fingers, how the smell of flowers and honey drifted up as he smoothed down her curls. He bent to examine the cut and held his breath.

"It's not bad," he said. "It doesn't need stitches…"

"You do humans now, too?"

"But," he continued as if she hadn't spoken, "you're going to have a goose egg."

Pink colored her cheeks. "Sorry to snap at you. I feel stupid."

He picked up one of her hands and took out another wipe. Gently he cleaned off the tip of each finger. "It's a good idea to move away before closing an overhead door."

She pulled a face. "I got that. Thanks."

He lifted her other hand and rubbed her fingertips. He marveled at the softness of her skin against his calloused palm, how pale her hands were for someone who lived in the southwest. Her fingernails were just this side of long, rounded at the tips but not painted. She'd kept them short when he knew her and usually stained with ink.

"Why are you being nice to me?"

"What?" He looked down to where her fingers were still laced in his.

A self-deprecating smile softened her mouth. "I know you don't want me here. In Brevia. Most of the town hates me for walking away from you, and the rest think I'm an idiot. No one wants me back."

"Your mother…"

"Needs someone to run the show for her event. I'm cheap labor, and I owe her for not being here the last time she needed me."

He squeezed her hands. "She doesn't blame you for your dad's death. You can't either."

"I can blame myself for a whole host of things that may or may not be my fault." Her brows drew down over her eyes. "Don't change the subject. I want to know why you keep rescuing me."

"Maybe I'm just a nice guy."

She stared at him.

"Or not." It burned his stomach to be so close to her. But here he was like a fly unable to resist the lure of the glowing blue light even when it expected the zap.

He didn't know how to answer her when he couldn't understand it himself. He needed to get away, head down to Charlotte and find a willing woman to scratch the itch that had started under his skin the moment he'd seen her in Carl's Diner. That would be the smart thing to do, the easy way out of a situation that could only end badly for both of them.

He tightened his grip on her fingers and drew her closer. He brought his face so close to hers that he could feel her warm breath against his skin. Still he didn't take her.

It's a test, he told himself. He measured his own resolve, his instinct for survival. *Let's see how much willpower I have, what I've learned in the past decade.* He was smarter now and knew enough to protect himself against the pain that

Lainey was bound to cause him. Seconds ticked by, and he wasn't sure if the pounding in his ears was his heart or hers.

I can do this.

I can let her go.

Her tongue snaked out and traced the seam of her lip. An involuntary gesture, he knew. But as soon as he saw the pink tip he was a goner.

What the hell, he thought and leaned in to kiss her. Just one time wouldn't mess him up that bad.

Ten years disappeared in the space of an instant. She might look and sound different, but Lainey Morgan tasted exactly like he remembered.

She tasted like home.

Lainey felt her eyes drift shut as Ethan's mouth brushed hers. She must have knocked her head really hard or this would never happen.

When a cart clattered nearby, the reality of the situation hit her, and she bolted up then grabbed the side of the Land Cruiser as stars exploded behind her eyes.

"Whoa, there." Ethan stood and steadied her.

"What were we thinking?" she said with a gasp, swatting away his arm. She pointed her finger at him. "What were *you* thinking? Anyone could have seen us."

"Don't start poking me again." He wrapped his palm around her finger and lowered her arm. "There are worse things that could happen."

"Not for me. Not in this town. We can't get involved." She paused. "For a lot of reasons."

His mouth thinned into a hard line. "It was a kiss. I didn't ask you to go steady. We're adults now. Things change."

That's where he was wrong. The jumble of emotions bouncing around her stomach sent a clear message that nothing had changed. "I just can't," she whispered.

"Is your head okay?"

She touched one finger to the scratch. "It's fine. No big deal."

"Put some ointment on it when you get home and call me right away if you get a headache or feel dizzy. I mean it. Anything out of the ordinary."

"I'm fine, Ethan," she repeated.

His hand lifted then pulled back. "Good night, Lainey."

She nodded and he turned and stalked across the parking lot to his truck.

She wanted to call after him but knew it wouldn't do any good. She rationalized the way her skin tingled by telling herself she hadn't had a decent date in over a year.

She was…the words desperate and hard up came to mind. Casual relationships were her forte, but it had become easier not to bother.

She wasn't going to bother now either. Not with Ethan. She had enough complications in her life without looking for more.

"I ran into Lainey the other day."

"Hmm."

"Have you seen her? She looks great—grown up in all the right places."

Ethan took a long swig of beer and studied Tim Reynolds over the bottle. He knew Tim and Lainey had been friends in high school, so it didn't surprise Ethan that Tim had seen her. But it still got under his skin to discuss Lainey in that way. "Did you come here to gab or watch the game?"

Dave Reynolds, Ethan's best friend and Tim's older brother, grabbed a third slice of meat lovers from the pizza box on the coffee table. With his cropped hair and stocky build, Dave still looked every bit the defensive lineman he'd been in high school. "Where'd you see her?"

Tim's wary gaze switched from Ethan to Dave. "She came

into the newspaper office. Press stuff for her mama's event. I guess she's helping out since Vera's sick."

Ethan saw Dave's eyebrows lift. "Did you know, E?"

Ethan took the last swallow from his beer and dropped the empty bottle on the table. "Yeah, I knew." He turned his attention back to the Braves.

"So you've seen her?" Tim asked again.

Tim Reynolds was a persistent little twit, Ethan thought. Maybe that's what made him a good newspaper reporter. Although if he was that good he probably wouldn't have left the *Atlanta Journal-Constitution* to become the editor for *The Brevia Times*.

"I've seen her." He reached for another slice of pizza. "Her dog had some problems."

"Was it weird?" Dave asked.

"It ate a pair of underpants." He turned back to the game but realized both men stared at him.

"What?"

Dave shook his head. "Your job is foul. I meant was seeing Lainey weird?"

To Ethan, weird was the green fuzz that grew on leftovers in the back of his fridge. Seeing Lainey had been like free-falling off a cliff—exhilarating, mind-blowing and scary as hell. He liked his life the way he'd arranged it—simple and uncluttered. His friends accused him of caring more about the animals he treated than real people. That worked for Ethan. He wouldn't let Lainey complicate things again.

He took a deep breath to clear his mind. "It was fine."

"I'm going to talk to her for the paper. A success story piece—someone who actually made it out of Brevia and lived to tell the tale." Tim stood and picked up the empty pizza box. "Plus she's hot, huh?"

"Shut up, Tim," Ethan and Dave said in unison.

"What's the big deal? You said it was fine."

Before Ethan could answer, Dave said, "Hey, Tim, grab more beer from the garage, will ya?"

Tim watched Ethan but answered, "Sure thing, bro." He turned and headed through Dave's kitchen.

"Thanks," Ethan said when he'd disappeared.

"Sorry about that. I'm glad he's back home because it makes my mom happy, but sometimes I wonder how we came from the same parents. Tim can be kind of out there, you know?"

"He's okay."

Dave looked skeptical. "You've always been like a second brother to him—especially after you kept an eye on him in college. I still owe you for that. So how long is Lainey going to be in town?"

"The rest of the summer. She's taken over plans for the fundraiser and adoption fair. It's no big deal."

Dave whistled low. "You worked pretty close with Vera on last year's deal. Is it going to be the same with Lainey?"

Ethan thought about her soft lips under his and how sweet her breath had tasted in his mouth.

Nothing was the same with Lainey.

"We'll see," he said with a shrug. "Seriously, it's no big deal."

"This is me, E. I'm the one who found you knee-deep in take-out bags and beer cans a month after she ran off."

"I survived."

"Barely," Dave argued. "Dude, I thought you might go all Unabomber and hide out in the woods for the rest of your life."

"I was young and stupid."

Dave shoved the last bite of pizza crust into his mouth. "At least you're older now," he said around a mouthful.

"Thanks for the vote of confidence."

Tim came into the room holding three beers. "What's going on?"

"Nothing," Ethan and Dave answered at the same time.

"Whatever," Tim mumbled as he handed each of them a bottle.

Ethan knew Tim felt like the third wheel, but right now he didn't care. He was glad for the quiet. Atlanta came to bat at the top of the seventh inning. Ethan sank against the cushions and watched the Braves try to even the score. Framed photos of his friend's two young daughters and wife filled the shelves around the flat screen.

Ten years ago Ethan had imagined this life for himself—a couple of kids and a wife. He'd expected Julia to be the woman in the pictures cradling his kids. That was how it was done in Brevia. Maybe that's why it had been so hard when Julia had taken off to New York City.

Lainey had brought him back to life. He sure hadn't planned on her getting pregnant the first time they'd been together. Hell, he hadn't even planned on being with her. Dating his ex-girlfriend's sister, that was the lowest of the low. But he couldn't help it—everything about Lainey had drawn him in.

She hadn't gotten pregnant on purpose. He'd known it even with the town trying to convince him otherwise. But it wouldn't have mattered. As soon as he'd found out about the baby, he'd been determined to create a better life than the one his messed-up family had given him. He was going to be the kind of father he'd wanted. The kind who took his kid fishing and not to the racetrack. The kind who grilled burgers on the patio while the kids played in the backyard, not one who sat in the darkened living room while the rest of the family tiptoed through the house, trying not to disturb him.

Ethan had never gotten that chance.

After a few rounds at the bar, guys would still slap his back and toast to how he'd dodged the marriage bullet. He'd smile and raise a glass but he never swallowed. He could not bring himself to drink to the absolute worst day of his life.

He stood, setting his still-full bottle on the table. "I've got a long day tomorrow," he said as he stood, wiping his palms against the sides of his cargo shorts.

Dave stretched his arms over his head. "Me, too. I want to get the walls up on the Perry Park building before Vicki gets back."

Dave owned the largest commercial construction company in the county. His business was thriving thanks to the recent influx of residents wanting to escape to the mountains.

"I drove by last week. At this rate you'll be done by end of summer."

"How's your place coming?"

Ethan shrugged. "I'm hoping to be in by Labor Day."

"I should have a couple weekends to help out."

"I'd appreciate that."

"I can help, too," Tim said as he finished another beer.

"Sure, bud."

Tim's eyes narrowed and his voice grew loud. "That crap with the chain saw was not my fault."

"You cut through my front door."

"The damn thing got away from me. Could've happened to anyone."

Ethan smiled. "You bet."

Tim sprang out of the chair and around the coffee table. "You think I can't handle some stupid power tool." He shoved his palms into Ethan's chest. "Are you saying I'm not good enough to build your high and mighty house?"

"Dude." Dave rose from the couch. "Chill."

Ethan crossed his arms and stared at Tim. The other man's cheeks were red with anger, but his eyes didn't quite focus.

"How many beers have you had?" Ethan asked.

Tim used the sleeve of his T-shirt to wipe the side of his mouth. "A few," he mumbled. "Who are you—my mother?"

Ethan tilted his head toward the front door. "Let me drive you home. You can get your car in the morning."

Tim hesitated then glanced at Dave. "Fine." He wobbled to the front door and let himself out without looking back.

"Thanks for taking care of him," Dave said.

"You'd do the same for me. Hell, you did the same for me. I'm not going to lose it like that ever again."

Dave nodded then settled back onto the couch. "You better get out there. I don't want him taking a leak on my shrubs."

Ethan grinned. "See ya later, buddy."

They didn't speak as Ethan drove toward Tim's apartment in the north end of town.

"Sorry I flew off the handle back there," Tim said, breaking the silence as Ethan pulled to a stop at the curb.

"No worries," Ethan answered, tired and ready to crawl into his own bed.

"I've been stressed at work. Maybe I need to let off a little steam."

Ethan let his eyes drift shut. "I know the feeling."

As Tim opened the door of the truck's cab, light flooded the interior.

"Hey, Tim?"

The other man looked over his shoulder. "Yeah?"

"Even stressed-out, don't start something you can't finish. It'll just cause trouble."

Tim's back went rigid, and Ethan saw his knuckles tighten around the door handle. "Sure thing, E. I got it." He climbed out of the truck and slammed the door shut.

Ethan drove away thinking about how his night had gone to hell so fast. After seeing Lainey in the parking lot, he'd wanted a distraction, and watching the game at Dave's had seemed as good as any. Then Tim had opened his big mouth about Lainey and how good she'd looked. Tension knotted in Ethan's stomach at the thought of another guy looking at Lainey, kissing her the way he had.

Do not go there.

He eased his foot off the gas pedal. This time of night, the only thing he'd run into on the dark road leading to the clinic was a random deer, but he didn't want to take chances. He rolled down the window and let the air calm his boiling blood.

How hard could it be to deal with Lainey for the summer? Hell, he might not see her much. Between the clinic and his house he could stay plenty occupied. He'd pawn off most of his responsibilities for the adoption fair to Steph. Then Lainey would be gone and his life would get back to normal.

By the time he started down the long dirt driveway toward the clinic, he felt more in control. More like the practical man he'd worked to become.

He swung the truck in next to the converted trailer where he currently lived. Something near the door caught in the glow of his headlights. He turned on the brights and leaned over the steering wheel to get a better look. Then realized he was looking directly at a woman's shapely backside. A string of expletives exploded from Ethan's mouth as the figure turned.

In the glare of his lights, she shaded her eyes with her forearm. Still, Ethan would have known the halo of curls that cascaded around Lainey's shoulders anywhere.

She was the last person he'd want to see standing on his front porch this late at night.

At least that's what he told himself.

Chapter Six

Cutting the brights, he climbed out of the truck. In the porch light, she looked as much like a deer in headlights as anything that would have crossed his path.

"What are you doing here?" His voice sounded rough in his own ears.

"I didn't…you weren't…" She whirled around to the front step then turned toward him. "Here," she said, pushing a plate into his stomach.

His hands curled around the sides of it, brushing her fingers in the process. She snatched back her hands.

"It's my way of saying thank you," she said, her voice quiet. "For helping Pita. What happened earlier…well, I don't know exactly what happened." She hugged herself and looked away. "But I still want to thank you. So there. I made brownies."

Ethan quirked a brow. "You bake now?"

"They're from a box," she said with a frown then added, "but they're good. I had one on the way over."

"I see that." He reached forward and with one finger flicked a chocolate crumb from her bottom lip.

Big mistake. Just that tiny contact with her made his insides explode like the night sky on the Fourth of July. Once again, all thoughts of being practical drained from his head.

She looked so beautiful standing in front of him, backlit by the hazy glow of the porch light. She wore a pair of cotton shorts and a faded blue tank top. While some women went to great lengths with hair, makeup and fancy clothes, Lainey never needed to try that hard.

To Ethan, she'd always looked best when she was natural— half awake and curled in his arms in the morning or fresh out of the shower, her hair damp. Or like now with a smudge of chocolate on her face, curls flying around her head.

He lifted one long strand. "I used to love your hair."

She smacked at his hand. "Don't do that."

"What?"

"I can't think straight when I'm near you." She blew out a huffy breath. "You're messing with my mind. I just wanted to give you brownies."

He glanced at his watch. "And you *had* to bring them over at eleven o'clock? It couldn't wait for morning?"

She shifted from one foot to the other. "I needed to get out of the house," she said, not meeting his gaze. "It's too quiet without Mom. Weirds me out."

"Do you want to come in for a bit?"

Her eyes widened. "I didn't come here for *that*."

"I wasn't talking about *that*," he said, exasperated. "A cup of coffee, that's all. Trust me, Lainey, I'm happy with my life just the way it is."

She shook her head. "I'm okay. The drive over here calmed me down." Her brows rose as her chin lifted. "Why are you home so late? Hot date?"

ainey's hackles rose and she took a deep breath. "I don't
k we've met." She extended a hand. "I'm Lainey Mor-
Vera's daughter."

he girl reluctantly shook Lainey's hand. "I know who
are."

he butterflies in Lainey's stomach multiplied into a full
y. *Get a grip,* she told herself. This girl's censure was the
of the iceberg. She expected much worse from the com-
tee members in this morning's meeting. She'd managed to
e out at the hospital or her mother's house since she'd been
own, only venturing to the grocery store under the cover
darkness. Today she'd finally be exposed to the light and
bright glare of angry feelings that came with it.

Squaring her shoulders, she offered the girl her brightest
ile. "What's your name?"

'Brandy Lott. I'm a temp because the regular receptionist
to do office management stuff over at the shelter. We're
t-staffed with Vera gone."

I'm sure everyone is grateful to have you here."

hesitant look lit Brandy's kohl-rimmed blue eyes. "I
know. The phones get really busy. I've only been here
ek. I still drop lots of calls."

Happens to everyone."

andy looked hopeful. "You really think so?"

iney nodded. She didn't think so but was determined
ke an ally of this girl. "We're in the same boat. I've got
my mom's big event, and I'm totally at a loss. Since
on the front lines, I'd appreciate any suggestions you
She paused. "And if there's anything you need, I'm
o help."

girl peered over the top of the tall counter toward
y. "Actually," she said in a hushed tone, "I had a Big
the way in. Could you watch the phones while I run
throom?"

He grinned. "Maybe."

"Who's the…uh…lucky girl?"

His smile widened. "Wouldn't you like to know?"

She huffed again and kicked the toe of her shoe into the
dirt. "I couldn't care less."

"Yeah, right."

She rolled her eyes and Ethan felt something he didn't want
to name unfurl in his stomach. Damn. This is how it had always been with Lainey—too easy. Long conversations late at
night, the quick banter back and forth. She made it too easy
to remember how much he liked being near her. Too easy to
forget how she'd ruined his life long ago. She was only here
for the summer before she left again, taking another big chunk
of his heart with her if he wasn't careful.

"Well, thanks for the brownies," he said and started to
move past her.

She stopped him with her hand on his forearm, her palm
cool against his skin.

"Ethan?" Her voice was hesitant, barely a whisper.

"Yeah?"

"Do you think I can handle everything for the adoption
event?"

"What do you mean—"

"I've disappointed my mom so many times. I'm a regular
expert at not living up to her expectations. I don't want to
mess this up, too."

"Listen to me, Lainey, because I'm only going to say this
once. You'll do great."

"Will you help me? I know it's awkward, but I've gone
through the files from last year. You worked on every piece.
I'm not sure I can do it without you."

He could tell how much it took out of her to ask for help. It was not her nature. Lainey was a giver. That's how it had been for him. When they'd been together all those years ago, he didn't have anything to offer her. But she hadn't cared. She'd saved his miserable life and he'd ruined hers. He couldn't turn his back on her.

"Of course I'll help." He dragged in a breath through his mouth, trying to clear his lungs.

"Thank you," she whispered. She pulled her hand away and stepped back. "Mama's using the clinic conference room as her base of operations, right?"

"Yep."

"I'll be there in the morning. Good night, Ethan."

He waited until she was safely in the SUV before he turned for his door. As far as he knew, no one in Brevia locked up their houses at night. He let himself into the darkened trailer and without turning on the lights, set the plate on the coffee table and sank onto the couch. Josie, the clinic's resident cat, nudged her head against his arm.

He owed Lainey his help, he reasoned. He'd played a big part in the decisions that led to her estrangement from her mother. He knew Vera, like most of the town, had condemned Lainey for going after him. But their attraction had been mutual. She may have had a crush on him before he noticed her, but she never would've acted on her feelings if he hadn't made the first move.

Ten years later, most of the longtime residents of Brevia still blamed her for breaking up small town "Ken & Barbie." Blamed her for that and so much more. His relationship with Julia had been nothing compared to what he'd felt for Lainey. Everyone wanted to help Vera, but Ethan could make it easier by giving Lainey his public support.

He wondered what it would cost him in the end.

* * *

Lainey recognized the feeling of butterflies ach. Each new assignment, whether photographi on their annual migration across the Gobi Des zlies at the spring salmon runs in Alaska, brou same familiar flutter. Would she be good enoug wings flapping in her midsection teased? Would right shot?

Invariably, the worry subsided once she picked u era. Looking at the world through the lens remaine sonal brand of meditation. She saw her surrounding the naked eye missed. Just the feel of the camera's v her hands, her finger on the shutter, relaxed her. feel safe.

This morning Lainey didn't have a camera to h As she walked through the clinic's entrance, her offered no protection from the stares and whis come.

She felt better after talking with Ethan last set her off balance in another way. Baking brov thing, but what had possessed her to deliver the he'd promised to support her, a fact that gave fidence today.

Several people sat in the waiting area as ward the reception desk.

"Is Dr. Daniels around?" she asked the seated at a computer on the other side of a

"He got called out to the Johnsons' farm eyes on the computer screen. "An emergen there someone else who can help?" She pu the computer and looked up.

Lainey saw recognition dawn in the g shoulders stiffened and her eyes narrowed with him anyway?" she asked, suspicio

to
to
you
have
happ
Th
the lo
Gulp
to the

Lainey hadn't been behind the reception desk since she'd graduated from high school. "I guess," she answered slowly.

Brandy grinned. "Thanks. I'll be quick as a lick."

Lainey eased around the side of the counter and through the door that led to the front office.

Brandy stood and pointed at a complex-looking phone system. "Just hit the button when the light blinks."

Lainey didn't have time to ask what she should say to the caller. Brandy disappeared through the doorway that led to the back of the clinic.

Within seconds, a green light next to the 'one' button began to blink and a muted ring broke the quiet.

With a groan, Lainey picked up the receiver and pressed the flashing light. "All Creatures Animal Hospital. May I help you?" The phone system may have changed but the words rolled off her tongue easily. She'd answered the clinic's phone every summer and Saturday mornings for most of her teen years.

She forced her attention back to the task at hand and realized the other end of the phone remained silent.

"Hello? May I help you?"

"Lainey?"

Unexpected heat rushed to her cheeks. "Ethan?"

"Lainey," he repeated, his voice rough. "Why are you answering the phone?"

"I got here early. Brandy's in the bathroom."

She heard a muttered curse through the line. "The meeting isn't for another forty-five minutes."

"I know." She sighed. "I wanted time to get my bearings and prepare before the old battle-axes show up."

He laughed, and her resident butterflies took flight again for different reasons.

"Are you nervous?"

"Of course not," she said quickly.

Silence.

"Maybe a little," she amended. "You're going to be here, right?"

"That's why I'm calling." His voice was quiet. "The situation with the mare is more serious than I thought."

"Oh." Her stomach sank.

"You'll do great. Remember the old trick—imagine Mrs. Vassler and her cronies in their skivvies. It's the great equalizer."

Lainey smiled a bit. It was the same advice he'd given her ten years ago before an oral presentation she'd had in one of her art history courses. Back then all she'd wanted was to get through her classes so she could spend time with Ethan. She could not have cared less about how she did on a speech.

This morning mattered. This time she cared about getting it right.

She glanced at the desk. "I need to go. Lines two and three are flashing."

"Be sure to—"

She didn't hear what he said as she slammed down the receiver and picked it up again. She put line two on hold just as an older man leaned over the counter.

"I need to check in," he told her.

She held up one finger then pressed line two, putting them on hold, as well. She looked over her shoulder to see Brandy at the edge of the reception area, Stephanie Rand at her elbow.

"Help," she mouthed silently.

She stood and stepped away as the two women hustled forward. Brandy picked up the phone as Steph spoke to the man across the counter.

A moment later Steph turned and jerked her head toward the back of the clinic. Lainey followed her into the hall.

"What are you doing out there?" Steph whispered.

Lainey blew out a breath. "I have no idea. Brandy had to go to the bathroom," she said by way of an explanation.

"This place isn't a game, Lainey," Steph answered, her voice tight. "It's a much bigger operation than when your dad ran it."

"I'm sorry." Lainey pressed against the wall and put her hands on her knees, letting her head loll forward. Adrenaline and nerves pumped through her body, making her tingle. "I was trying to be nice. To make friends. It would be great if one person in this town didn't turn up their nose the minute I walked into the room."

Steph's tone softened. "Does that really happen?"

Lainey nodded, finding it difficult to speak.

"I don't think it's personal."

Lainey glanced up. "Are you kidding? How is that possible?"

"Everyone wants to protect Ethan. He's a huge part of this community. As much as your dad was back in the day."

Lainey straightened. "It's not a big deal, I guess. I want to have a look around before the meeting."

"I'll introduce you to the staff. Most of them are new to the area."

"So they won't hate me on sight?"

"You're kind of a legend around here."

Lainey groaned.

"Let's see what we can do to make you some new friends."

A half hour later, Lainey stood in an empty conference room, her mind reeling. Growing up, she'd spent so much time at the clinic, but what she'd seen today bore little resemblance to the animal hospital she remembered. She'd met the three other vets who worked with Ethan as well as several technicians.

Everyone had been friendly, and the energy that radiated from the entire building went beyond positive. Even the ani-

mals kenneled in back seemed okay with being in their cages.
Two different labs with various computers and high-tech sur-
gical equipment took up most of the building's rear. Each of
the six exam rooms, including the one she'd been in with
Pita, were enlarged and renovated from her days at the clinic.

"Here you go."

Lainey turned as Steph walked into the room and handed
her a cup of steaming coffee.

"Thanks." She cradled the mug between her palms and
took a sip. "I can't get over how things have changed. I knew
the clinic had expanded and about the addition of the shelter.
Seeing it firsthand…" She shook her head. "It's amazing."

Steph nodded. "Ethan had a vision."

Lainey propped one hip on the conference table. "I never
understood why he stayed. The whole reason he switched
from med school to the vet program was because of the baby.
Less time in school and my parents could help. Once that burden lifted I figured he'd be long gone."

"He felt a big responsibility to your mom and dad."

"What?" Lainey's brows furrowed. "Why?"

Steph held up her hands, palms open at Lainey's outraged
response. "I could be wrong. He was pretty much the reason
both you and your sister took off for good that summer. You
always loved it here, and Julia might have stuck around after
she came back from the big city. Who knows? But I think he
wanted to make amends for breaking up your family."

Lainey brought her fingers to her lips. "So Juls and I
moved on, and he got stuck paying for all our mistakes."

"I don't think he felt stuck. Not everyone was as hell-bent
on getting away from Brevia as you and your sister."

Lainey gave a sad laugh. "All I ever wanted was to spend
my life here. I never imagined leaving until the moment I
pulled out of the church parking lot."

"You never looked back," Steph countered.

"At what? All my dreams died that day at the hospital." She swallowed against the emotions rising in her throat.

"What about new dreams?"

Lainey forced herself to inhale. "Mine don't involve this town."

"Or Ethan?"

Lainey straightened the pile of papers that sat on the table next to her. "I need to pull it together before this meeting," she said as she stood, reaching into her purse for a tissue to wipe her running nose.

Steph's arms wrapped around her. She turned and hugged her old friend.

"I'm glad you're here."

"You may be the only one."

Steph gave Lainey's arms a tight squeeze. "A bunch of us are going to Cowboys Saturday night. Why don't you come?"

Lainey remembered the neon sign outside the bar she'd seen on her way into town. "Cowboys. Seriously?"

"There's line dancing." Steph grinned. "You own boots?"

"I actually *live* in the Southwest. Of course I own boots."

"Eight-thirty then."

Lainey grimaced. "Steph, I don't—"

A high-pitched "hello" interrupted her.

Five women ranging in age from thirty-five to a hundred and twenty filed in.

"That's my cue," Steph said quickly and walked out of the room, nodding greetings as she left.

"Good morning, Melanie," one of the older women said as she stepped forward.

"How are you, Mrs. Vassler?"

Ida Vassler looked at the group taking seats around the room and then to Lainey again. She'd been a fixture in Brevia since Lainey could remember. Her husband had owned the car dealership out on Route Four, and according to local

legend, had left Ida more money than God when he'd died.
Money she'd used to wield control over a variety of civic ac-
tivities—Vera's adoption fair included.

"Frankly, my dear," Ida said in a stage whisper loud enough
for the whole room to hear, "I'm a little worried."

Lainey took a step back and did a mental eye roll. "Really?"

"I'm not sure you have what it takes to make your mother's event a success."

"Well…I…" Lainey began but the older woman kept
speaking.

"In these tough times, I don't know if I want to put my
money behind an event that isn't going to be top-notch." Ida
patted Lainey's hand and gave her an insincere smile. "You
understand I'm sure."

For the briefest moment, Lainey wanted to run from the
room, flee this one-horse town like she'd done a decade earlier. But she wasn't that scared young girl anymore and no
one, especially not a leathery old biddy, could scare her off.

Heat flooded her cheeks, but she returned Ida's smile. "It's
sad that you'd let your animosity toward me get in the way
of helping animals who need it." She squeezed Ida's ample
arm. "Mama will be so disappointed."

A buzz broke out in the room. Ida's heavily rouged cheeks
turned an unfortunate shade of purple.

"Why you little—"

"I hope I'm not late," a low voice rang out through the
commotion.

Ethan's large body filled the doorway. He met her heated
gaze and nodded slightly. Relief shot through her.

He lifted a flat box into the air. "I picked up the muffins
you asked for, Lainey."

"Thanks." She hadn't said a thing about muffins.

He walked forward, greeting each of the women in the

room by name, the epitome of aw-shucks Southern charm. His accent sounded thicker than normal, his vowels a slow caress.

"I'm not sure I can eat even one." Reaching around Ida, he enveloped Lainey in a quick, friendly hug. "I had a couple of your brownies this morning. They've pretty much spoiled me for anything else." He winked at her. "Was that your mama's recipe?"

"Betty Crocker," Lainey whispered.

He threw his head back and laughed—a deep, rich sound that made her think of warm syrup sliding over a stack of pancakes. Lainey gazed around the room at the starry-eyed looks of every single woman.

Ida's eyes widened as she chewed on the inside of her cheek.

"Did I miss anything?" Ethan asked as he stepped away.

Her skin tingled from where she'd pressed against him, but Lainey forced a relaxed tone. "Mrs. Vassler may not sponsor the adoption fair. Tough economic times, you know."

"Right." Ethan nodded. "How's that guesthouse coming on your property, Miz Vassler?"

"Just fine, Ethan." Ida spoke through clenched teeth.

Lainey made her smile sympathetic. "Luckily, I spoke to a friend of mine at *National Geographic* last night. They want to do a feature on the event for their kids' magazine. I'm sure I could get them to offer a sponsorship."

Ethan let out a low whistle. "Your mother would sure appreciate that kind of exposure."

"But…wait…I didn't say…" Ida sputtered.

"Why don't you sit down, Mrs. Vassler," Lainey said sweetly. "We'll discuss this during the meeting."

The older woman nodded and scurried to the conference table. Ethan held out a chair for her then took a seat, as well.

Lainey picked up the stack of agendas and began passing them out, feeling suddenly like she could handle anything this town threw at her. "Let's get started. We've got a lot to cover."

Chapter Seven

The automatic door at the front of the hospital slid open. Lainey walked out of the sweltering summer heat and into the cool lobby.

Julia stood near the entrance, a cell phone pressed to her ear. A man in blue scrubs tripped over a wheelchair coming off the elevator as he craned his neck to get a better look. Julia could turn more heads seven months pregnant than Lainey would covered head to toe in whipped cream and caramel syrup.

"Are you ready to head up?" Lainey asked when Julia was finished. She bounced on her toes, too exhilarated from her success that morning to indulge long in comparisons to her sister.

"Sure thing. How was the meeting?" Julia dug through her purse, her long hair draped over her cheek like a curtain.

"Pretty good once Ida Vassler pulled in her claws." They turned and walked toward the elevator. "Ethan was there,"

Lainey added quickly. "Probably more as a favor to Mom, but it helped."

"She'll be happy." Julia punched the elevator button.

"Do you think…" Lainey started then broke off when Julia finally met her gaze. "What's the matter?"

The elevator door opened but instead of getting on, Julia whirled and fled down a long hallway off the hospital's main lobby. Lainey followed her into the women's restroom.

Julia stood with her hands gripped on either side of a metal sink. She bent so far forward Lainey couldn't see her face, but in the mirror's reflection tears dripped off the tip of Julia's nose.

"What happened?"

"Hormones," Julia said around a gulp. "I'm fine. I just need a minute."

"Liar." Lainey's voice echoed in the small space. "This has something to do with that phone call. Is everything all right with the baby?" Lainey's heart hammered in her chest, her eyes riveted to Julia's stomach.

Julia grabbed a wad of paper towels from the dispenser and blew her nose. "Are we alone?"

Lainey checked under each stall. "Yes."

"I tried to register for Lamaze class." Julia dabbed at her cheeks.

"So? That's what pregnant women do."

"They won't let me. I don't have a coach."

"You said Jeff is coming when his research wraps up. It won't be long now."

Julia's face crumbled, and she covered it with her hands. "I did a bad thing," she said between sobs.

Lainey wasn't sure what to do. She'd never seen her sister like this. She took a hesitant step forward and reached out to touch Julia's elbow.

"It'll be okay. Once Jeff gets here—"

Julia rubbed her hands over her face. "Jeff didn't go to Brazil for the summer. He took a job there. He's gone."

Lainey's brows drew together. "What about you and the baby?"

"You really didn't get pregnant to trap Ethan, did you?"

Relief skittered across the back of Lainey's neck. She wanted to think it didn't matter that anyone believed her. But it did. It always had. "No. I would never—"

"Well, I did. And it blew up in my face."

Lainey's jaw went slack. "You...why?"

"We dated for three years. I followed him from New York to Boston to Columbus. Anywhere work took him. But he wouldn't commit, wouldn't marry me." Julia's eyes glistened with unshed tears. "I gave him an ultimatum. That's when he told me he'd taken a research position in Brazil. He knew I wouldn't go with a baby." Her smile was sad. "Smooth move, huh?"

The floor shifted under Lainey's feet as her whole world started to spin. "Why haven't you told anyone?"

"Come on, Lainey. I was so mad at you for stealing Ethan. But when Jeff wouldn't give me what I wanted, I figured it worked for you, why not me?"

Lainey shook her head. "I didn't steal Ethan and it didn't work for me. He felt like he *had* to marry me and I couldn't live with that. I couldn't force him into a life he didn't want when he would have ended up with you if he'd had a choice."

"Do you still believe that?" Julia asked.

"Don't you?" Lainey shot back.

"You say he was forced, but he had a choice."

Right. Ethan was one of the good ones. No matter how much he'd hurt her, Lainey couldn't forget she'd brought it on herself. "What are you going to do now?"

"Do they have escort services for baby daddies?" Julia gave a harsh bark of laughter.

"Isn't there someone else?" Fear rose in Lainey's belly as Ethan's face flashed through her mind.

"I was going to tell Mom, ask for her help but—"

"Mom doesn't know?"

"No one knows," Julia said, her voice flat. "You're the only one I've told."

"I could help." Lainey looked around the bathroom, wondering who'd said those words. She *had* looked under the stalls, right?

"You'd do that for me?"

No way. Don't do it. You have to get the heck out of this town. "I can make it work."

"It wouldn't be too weird?"

Getting beamed up by the mother ship was weird. This was downright suicidal. "I know I'm not your favorite person in the world, but if you need me I'm here."

Tears welled in her sister's big eyes. "Thank you."

The restroom door opened and a middle-aged woman walked in, pausing as she caught sight of Lainey and Julia. She raised her eyebrows then shuffled into one of the stalls.

Lainey stepped up to a sink. "Can we get out of here?" she asked, using her fingertips to splash lukewarm water on her face.

Julia nodded.

As Lainey reached for a paper towel, Julia's arm wrapped around her shoulder. "I can't tell you how much you're saving my life right now. To feel like I'm not alone…it means everything."

Lainey hugged her back. She couldn't remember another time when she'd hugged her sister. Not once. It felt strange but somehow right.

The toilet flushed and Julia moved away. "Enough bonding in the bathroom. Let's go."

Lainey punched the elevator button for the third floor,

wondering if she was having some sort of out-of-body experience. She'd just agreed to be her sister's birthing coach. She was going to help Julia with her breathing, calm her nerves. Be there every step of the way. Including the delivery room. The actual birth and the blood. All of it.

Her stomach lurched and not from the elevator's movement. She saw Julia glance at her and tried to keep her features calm. She'd seen a few live births with animals while on assignment, and even that had overwhelmed her. It was too much—having it right in front of her face. It was so…real.

Not a great trait in a nature photographer. She could handle death—watching a pride of lions take down a wildebeest didn't faze her. A cub coming into the world was another story. Too big a reminder of what she'd never have.

How much harder would it be with her sister's baby?

"Are you coming?"

Lainey blinked and saw Julia standing outside the elevator, one hand holding back the sliding door.

She stepped into another hospital corridor. "I brought the nail polish she wanted."

"Ah, spa day." Julia patted her large tote bag. "I have stuff for facials. And my scissors."

Lainey's heart pumped the tiniest bit faster. "Your scissors?"

"Mom told me I'm cutting your hair."

"I don't know…"

Julia shrugged one shoulder. "It's up to you."

"I've worn my hair like this since sixth grade," Lainey said, fingering one long lock.

Julia grinned. "That's sort of the point."

"But it's so curly. What if I end up looking like Shirley Temple? Or maybe you don't remember my third grade picture."

In front of Vera's room, Julia turned. "Give me a little credit, would you?"

"Sorry," Lainey mumbled, still not convinced she needed to change her hairstyle. Then she remembered Ethan's warm hands when he'd held her head and said he'd loved her hair, making it so hard for her to keep distant from him.

She sucked in a breath as sparks danced across her belly. "You're right." She pushed open the door. "Cut it all off."

The smell of cheap cologne and stale beer assaulted her as she walked into Cowboys two nights later. Her fingers fluttered up to rub her bare neck. Although she'd cut almost six inches, true to her word Julia had given Lainey layers that somehow made her typically errant corkscrews relax into soft ringlets around her face. It just wasn't her. Or who she used to be.

Even her clothes felt different. Tonight she wore a sleeveless jersey-knit top and a dark blue miniskirt with a pair of black cowboy boots.

It was only nine o'clock but already a decent-size group of people crowded around the large bar that spanned the length of the room. On the walls, neon beer signs mixed with concert posters for various country singers, mostly Willie Nelson and Toby Keith. A dozen couples two-stepped around the wide wood-plank dance floor to a popular country ballad she recognized but couldn't quite name.

She scanned the crowd for a familiar face, but her gaze caught on an oversize mechanical bull in the corner, surrounded by what looked like a bed of stuffed potato sacks.

"You ever ridden one?" a voice asked close to her ear. She jumped what felt like ten feet then whirled to find Tim Reynolds at her side.

"Geez, Tim. Are you trying to give me a heart attack?" Adjusting her purse tighter against her side, she said, "No,

I've never ridden a bull—mechanical or otherwise. I saw them run once."

He blinked.

"You know, in Barcelona." She forced a smile. "I'm a little out of my element here. You're not helping by staring at me."

"Sorry. I still can't get over how great it is to see you. But where's your hair?"

"Julia cut it." She tried to hide her irritation. Tim had been her friend forever. He'd been the last person she'd seen before leaving Brevia and had been kind to her when she'd needed it most. She'd run into him a few times since coming back but found it difficult to slip into the easy camaraderie of youth. Maybe his time away from Brevia had changed him. Or maybe the change was in her. But something no longer fit.

"It looked better longer, like you wore it in high school."

"I've grown up." She blew out a breath. "It was time for my style to do the same. I travel too much for my job to fuss with long hair."

"I'd like to get out of town more." He took a drink of his beer. "I'm thinking of trying freelance magazine work. Running the paper is great, but I miss digging into research, interviewing sources. Nothing that would take me away too long, but I want the chance to do in-depth reporting. Something that really matters, like the work you do."

"That's exciting." She tried to focus on him while scanning over his shoulder for someone she recognized. "What did you have in mind?"

"Maybe *National Geographic*. We could coordinate a piece together. I'd love to take you out to dinner to get your advice. We have so much in common, Lainey. We always have."

"Oh." She didn't know how to answer. Tim had been a good friend. She supposed the least she owed him was dinner, but something about the look in his eye told her he wanted more than she could give him. "That would be fun," she said, thinking it sounded lame.

He didn't seem to notice. "Awesome. It's a date then."

She shifted under his gaze. "Have you seen Steph? I'm supposed to meet her."

He shook his head. "I want you to know something—"

At that moment a familiar voice rang out through the crowd. "Lainey, over here!"

Lainey looked around Tim to see Steph waving a leopard-print cowboy hat from one of the tables near the bar.

"There she is." Lainey breathed a sigh of relief.

"Great," Tim said, his tone disappointed. "I'll see you later."

Lainey had a vision of Tim walking through the high school hallways alone. He'd had trouble finding his place. She could sympathize now as much as she did then. "A few people from the clinic are getting together," she said on a whim. "Do you want to go over with me?"

His face brightened. "Are you sure? I don't want to be a fifth wheel."

Lainey knew all too well what it felt like to not fit in. "I'm sure."

She wound her way through the people until she found Steph.

"Hey, lady," Steph hollered above the music. "It's Saturday night. Let's start this party." She did a little shimmy with her hips then tugged Lainey into a hug.

Lainey laughed. It was the same line Steph had used every weekend during high school. Exhilaration hummed through Lainey at being part of the mix.

Several groups of clinic staff stood around two tall bar tables. She greeted people and drew Tim forward, making introductions.

"You know Tim," she said, turning to Steph.

"Sure." Steph's eyes widened just a touch. "You need a drink, girl." She grabbed Lainey by the arm and yanked her to the bar. "Are you with him?"

"With Tim?" She laughed. "No. I ran into him when I got here."

"Good. You need to keep your options open."

I don't have options, Lainey thought.

Then Steph gestured with two fingers toward the bartender. "I'm so excited you're here."

"Me, too." Lainey smiled, letting her mind drift from Tim. "Thanks for not holding a grudge that I haven't kept in touch."

"What happened to you sucked." Steph leaned forward to plant a kiss on Lainey's cheek. "I might have flipped out, too, if I'd been in your shoes."

Flipped out? Lainey had never thought of her reaction to events of that summer in those terms. She'd simply left, moved on with her life without looking back.

Or had she? She'd made something out of her professional life, but it was a different story on the personal front. She had a couple of friends at a gallery in Santa Fe, but they were more business associates.

The longest she'd had a boyfriend in the past decade had been about seven months, mostly via phone and email because of her travel schedule. She'd ended it as soon as he'd started talking about the future and a family.

She knew the truth ten years ago. She was far too broken for anyone to want to be with her. She wouldn't take the chance of trusting another man with her heart. *Ever.*

She looked down as Steph pushed a tall glass into her hand. "What's this?"

"A Cowboy Kamikaze." Steph wiggled her eyebrows. "The house specialty."

"I'm not much of a drinker," Lainey said with a grimace, eyeing the frozen concoction.

"Try it," Steph urged.

With one finger, Lainey pushed the paper umbrella out of the way and took a tentative sip from the straw. Smooth, sweet liquid slid over her tongue. "It doesn't taste like alcohol."

"A spoonful of sugar makes the medicine go down." Steph winked. "In the most delightful way." She held her glass aloft. "To old friends and new adventures."

Lainey clinked her glass against Steph's. "To old friends," she repeated.

Both women sucked on their straws then Steph nodded toward the front of the bar. "I can't believe it. Ethan's here."

Lainey's swallow caught in her throat. She sputtered and blinked back tears. "I didn't know he was coming." It was hard to sound casual when she was choking.

Steph thumped on her back. "He usually doesn't—too difficult."

"Why?" Lainey took another drink to clear her throat. "Does he ride the bull?"

Steph laughed. "It's the women. They throw themselves at him."

Lainey's stomach landed with a thud near her feet. "Does he…"

"Ride the ladies?" Steph gave her a meaningful grin.

"Have a girlfriend?" Lainey finished.

"Nope. By now you'd think they'd realize all his time and energy go to the clinic."

Like picking a scab, Lainey couldn't help but continue. "He has to date sometimes."

Steph shook her head. "He's got a long line willing to help relieve his tension, if you know what I mean."

"He wanted a family. His own little football team."

"He volunteer coaches over at the elementary school," Steph countered.

"But—"

"Listen, Lainey, you weren't the only one who was scarred by what happened."

"I never said..." The music changed, drowning out her words.

"I love this song." Steph tapped her foot as Kenny Chesney began to sing about tractors being sexy.

Lainey took another drink only to suck up air from her straw. How had she finished so fast? She blamed her buzzing head on that and not Ethan.

"Come on." Steph pulled on her arm. "Let's dance."

Lainey lifted her empty glass. "I need another."

Steph's eyes widened a fraction before she threw back her head and laughed. "This night is going to be fantastic," she shouted, gliding through the crowd.

Chapter Eight

A muscle ticked in Ethan's jaw as he watched yet another guy gyrate up to Lainey on the dance floor. He'd hardly recognized her when he'd first seen her at the bar. Now he couldn't take his eyes off her.

Stephanie Rand grabbed her and executed some complicated spin to get Lainey away from her latest admirer. Lainey wiggled her hips, curls bouncing around her face as she laughed.

Ethan's gut clenched. She was gorgeous.

He rarely made an appearance at the limited but popular Brevia bar scene. When he'd heard from Steph that Lainey was going to be here, he'd decided to come.

Bad choice.

"I told you she was hot now."

Ethan pushed away from the table and resisted the urge to shove his fist into something as he turned to Tim Reynolds.

She was hot before, you fool, he said to himself. "You did," he answered, silently counting to ten and remembering his promise to his best friend to look out for his little brother.

Tim put down one beer and picked up another. "I asked her out."

Ethan's beer dropped to the table with a clank. "You did what?" On the dance floor, Lainey twirled and laughed.

Tim took a quick step back. "I didn't figure you'd care. She and I have a lot in common, and the two of you are ancient history, right?"

Ethan leveled a look at his supposed friend then ground out, "Right."

"She's been giving me some big-time signals since she got back."

Over the roar in his ears, Ethan heard the music change to a slow ballad. He didn't care, he told himself. Lainey meant nothing to him. He wanted to erase the debt he felt he owed her. Nothing more. If Tim could help with that, so be it.

Tim rubbed his palms together. "Here's my chance."

Ethan would have stopped him, but a hand clamped down on his shoulder. Paul Thie, the young vet he'd hired earlier this summer, stepped closer.

"Hey, boss," Paul said with his usual mile-wide grin. "This is awesome, huh? Reminds me of a few places in Amarillo."

Paul was a native Texan who'd interned with Ethan the past two summers before being hired two weeks ago. As he talked to the young man, Ethan watched the crowded dance floor. Couples clung to each other, women resting cheeks on the shoulders of their partners. He craned his neck to catch a glimpse of Lainey and Tim. When he finally did, his blood pressure skyrocketed.

Tim held her way too close. The other man's arms snaked around her middle while her fingers rested on the corners of his shoulders. Tim turned her with the music and leaned forward to whisper something in her ear. Her already huge eyes widened a fraction. She shook her head, and they disappeared again as the crowd shifted.

"I'll talk to you later, Paul," Ethan said, not waiting for a response as he strode toward the dance floor.

He elbowed his way through couples until he spotted Lainey's caramel curls. Although the song hadn't ended, she pushed away from Tim, who held tight to her wrist. Ethan practically threw another man into a wall trying to get to them.

"Mind if I cut in?" He tried to keep his voice even. Cowboys on a Saturday night was no place to make a scene. "For old times' sake."

He saw Lainey swallow. "Sure," she answered.

"No way," Tim said at the same time. "Our dance isn't over."

Ethan's mouth thinned. "It's over. *Now.*"

Tim let go of Lainey's arm but didn't step away.

"Remember what I said, buddy." Ethan didn't try to hide his anger. "Don't start something you can't finish."

Tim's eyes narrowed, but he turned away, knocking into several people as he stomped off.

Ethan felt curious eyes on them. Without a word, he put his arms around Lainey. To his surprise, she wrapped her hands around his neck without protest. The warmth of her body melded against his. Her hair tickled his chin as her head tilted closer to his neck. She didn't look at him, which was lucky since his blood was now pumping for a different reason.

"What was going on with you two?" he asked.

She sighed, placing her cheek against his shoulder. His heart caught in his chest at the intimacy of the gesture.

"We were talking about high school and then...I don't know. I think he may be drunk." Her finger traced the side of his jaw. "I remember that scar," she whispered, her mouth so close to his face he could feel her breath when she spoke. "I remember everything about you."

He leaned back and looked into her eyes.

She blinked several times and gave him a lopsided smile. "Are *you* drunk?"

She scrunched up her nose as her smile widened. "I don't get out much," she said with a giggle.

"Holy crap," he muttered. "You're drunk."

Her mouth pulled down at the corners. "Don't be a buzz-kill, Ethan. It's been a rough week. My mama's sick. I agreed to be my sister's birth coach. And I'm missing assignment after assignment because I'm stuck in a town where the only people who don't hate me are just waiting until I mess up so they'll have an excuse to *start* hating me."

"Your Sunday's going to be even rougher once that buzz wears off."

The song ended and the music changed to a fast dance tune. Lainey grabbed both his hands and shook them back and forth. "Wanna dance?" she cooed.

"I want to take you home." He hauled her toward the door.

"Are you putting the moves on me?" she asked, laughing.

He kept walking. "Absolutely not."

She tripped and landed against his back. "Has anyone ever told you you're a real party pooper?"

"I don't think so." He looked down into her face, her generous mouth curved into an irresistible pout, and felt his insides tighten.

He straightened her and put his arm around her waist to steady them both. "How much did you have to drink?"

"Not a lot. Two or three. I think. They were yummy."

She giggled again and he shook his head. "You're a cheap date."

"This is *not* a date," she said as they moved out the bar's front door on to the street. Night had fallen, cooling the temperature enough to make it almost pleasant.

"Tell me about it." He dropped his hand from her waist. "My truck's parked around the corner."

He started down the sidewalk then noticed she wasn't following.

She stood in front of Cowboys' entrance, light from the neon pink sign making her skin glow. She tipped her head to one side and studied him, her expression a mix of confusion and raw pain.

"Would you want to date me?" she asked, her voice so low he barely heard her.

He rubbed his hands across his face. How could he answer that? He'd wanted to marry her ten years ago and spend the rest of their lives together. They both knew he'd offered because of the baby, because that's what a boy from Brevia did when he got a girl pregnant. Who knew what would have happened if fate hadn't stepped in?

"Come on," he said by way of an answer. He held out a hand. "Let's go."

She crossed her arms over her chest. "I don't think…" she started before taking several wobbly steps toward the street. She caught herself on a lamppost before tumbling to the curb.

Ethan was at her side in an instant. "Lainey?"

She hung on to the streetlight like a life raft. "I need to go home," she whispered.

"I know, honey." He rubbed his palm against her back. "I can help you."

She raised her bright green eyes to his, still clinging to the pole. "You won't let me fall?"

"I won't let you fall."

Tentatively, she released one arm.

He leaned forward and wrapped it around his shoulder. "All the way now," he coaxed.

Her other hand slid around the lamppost, and he scooped her up. He heard a chorus of whoops and catcalls from the small huddle of smokers outside the bar.

She squirmed against him, trying to look over his shoulder. "How embarrassing," she mumbled. "I can walk, you know."

"I know," he agreed. "But give your feet a break after all the dancing."

She seemed to ponder that for a moment. "Good idea," she said and dropped her head against his chest.

He walked quickly to his truck, trying not to notice the feel of her rounded bottom pressed into his stomach. He didn't want to remember what it felt like to have her arms curled around him.

At the corner, he shifted her, pulling out his keys. Bending at an awkward angle, he opened the passenger door and deposited her as gently as he could. He reached over her to buckle the seat belt.

He tried to back out of the truck's cab, but she reached up, placing her cool fingers on either side of his face.

"I'm definitely drunk," she said with a lopsided smile.

He held his breath. "Yep."

"You could take advantage of me."

The air drained from his lungs. "Nope."

Her expression turned serious. "I could take advantage of you."

He closed his eyes. "You don't—"

Her mouth touched his and he froze. Her tongue traced the curve of his lips. He didn't move.

"Kiss me back," she whispered into his mouth.

And, God help him, he did.

He pushed his fingers through her short curls and slanted his mouth over hers, pressing her against the truck's leather seat. If ever there was a reminder that she'd left Brevia a girl and returned a woman, this kiss was it.

A very drunk woman.

He broke away, pressing his forehead to hers for several moments until he gained control. Her eyes didn't open, and a slight smile lifted one corner of her mouth.

"Lainey—"

She made a muffled sound.

"Lainey?" he repeated, realizing she was fast asleep.

She wiggled deeper into the leather. He adjusted the seat belt where it cut across her neck and closed the passenger door.

He shook his head and blew out a frustrated breath. "Woman, you are the worst thing ever to happen to my ego."

Lainey struggled to open one eye. She immediately regretted it as bright morning light pounded against her head, frying her few remaining brain cells.

"Owww." She pulled the covers all the way up.

After a few minutes, she tried again, driven by a bone-deep need for water and a handful of ibuprofen. Swinging her legs over the side of the bed, she sat up. The pounding in her head intensified, and she wondered if the percussion session behind her temple might actually find its way out.

A glass of water and bottle of pills sat on her nightstand. She washed down two orange pills with a long drink.

For a moment, she congratulated herself on having the foresight to leave them there. Then memories of the previous night rushed through her mind. Random images of Ethan, his hands on her, his breath on her skin.

She glanced down at the old T-shirt and boxers she wore. She could feel that her bra and underpants remained intact. That was a good sign, right?

Her outfit from the previous night was folded in a neat pile on the dresser. That was bad.

Her eyes shifted to the clock on the nightstand. Nine-thirty. She patted the empty space next to her. No Pita.

A noise from downstairs propelled her to her feet. The dog was used to eating by eight. Lainey couldn't take the chance on Pita getting into something else that would require veterinary services.

She walked down each step trying not to bounce or jostle any part of her body. "Pita," she called as she headed through the hallway. She winced as even that small noise exploded in her head.

In the kitchen she expected to find garbage strewn across the floor or food pulled out of the pantry—definitely not the sight that greeted her.

Ethan stood in front of her mother's old gas stove, stirring what looked to be a skillet full of eggs.

Several shopping bags sat on the tile counter. Pita lay sprawled under the kitchen table, her tail thumping.

Lainey rubbed at the crusted drool stuck to the side of her chin. "What are you doing?" Her mouth felt like it was stuffed with cotton.

Ethan glanced over his shoulder. "You're awake," he said, then turned his attention back to the stove. As if being in Vera's kitchen making breakfast on a Sunday morning was normal.

More than her aching head threw her off balance. She sucked in an irritated breath, but the scent of coffee brewing distracted her.

Following her gaze, Ethan gestured toward the coffeepot. "It's fresh."

She poured a big mug and took a drink. The hot liquid felt smooth on her dry throat. She prayed the caffeine would kick in quickly and tried to get a handle on what was going on in her mother's house. "You don't cook," she said, using her mug to point to the skillet.

"They're eggs, Lainey. Not exactly five-star."

"The only eggs you ever had were sandwiched between a McMuffin."

"I was in med school. No one cooks in med school."

That was one of the things he'd liked about her when they were together—how she'd cooked for him. It made him feel cared about he'd told her.

Lainey had taken the words to heart. She'd made sure the cupboards in her tiny dorm room were stocked with his favorite snacks. Anything to keep him coming around. Even when her soul ached for someone to love her for who she was and not because she made it so easy.

He chopped a handful of mushrooms and dropped them into the pan as the theme from *The Twilight Zone* played in her head. He stirred the eggs and lifted the lid on another fry pan.

"Is that bacon?"

"I thought you could use a greasy breakfast to soak up some of last night's demons," he answered, adjusting a knob on the front of the stove. "I got donuts, too."

"From Three Rivers?" She hadn't had anything from her favorite bakery in years.

He pointed to a box on the kitchen table. "A dozen jellies."

That news made her temporarily forget the strangeness of the morning. "My favorite."

"I remember," he murmured, his attention focused on the stove.

She sank into one of the ladder-back chairs that circled the table, still moving slowly although the coffee had numbed the pain to a dull ache.

Flipping open the cardboard box, she inhaled the sweet, doughy aroma. Her first bite was like returning to heaven and worth the ten-year wait. She licked out a dollop of jelly with her tongue and noticed Ethan watching her, his mouth tipped up on one side.

"Thanks," she said around a mouthful.

"Anytime." His voice was low.

A flush spread from her toes to the top of her head. She rubbed her feet against Pita's soft fur under the table.

"So did we…you know…?" she started, wanting to get the difficult conversation out of the way. She concentrated on the doughnut. "Parts of last night are fuzzy for me."

He set a plate piled high with a perfect omelet and several strips of bacon in front of her.

"Did we get down and dirty?" he prompted.

She glanced up, heat pouring into her cheeks. "These aren't my clothes from last night."

He took the chair across from her. "Let's see," he said, rubbing his chin. "Would that have been before or after you passed out in my truck?"

"What's wrong with me?" she asked with a groan. "I never get out of control."

He tapped her plate with his fork. "Eat your eggs and stop beating yourself up. It's been a crazy week. You let off a little steam—no big deal."

"You're doing it again."

"What?"

"Being nice."

He studied her over the rim of his coffee mug. "It makes me an idiot, I know. But do you want me to stop?"

Lainey couldn't answer that question so she took another bite. Her eyes drifted closed. The omelet was perfect—light and creamy with the perfect mix of veggies and cheese. "This is so good." It tasted familiar. "How did you—"

"Your mom."

Her forked stopped midbite.

He shrugged. "I hung around here at mealtime for so many years, she eventually made me learn a few things. It was a lot better than being with my dad. And since my mom left…"

Lainey thought about what Steph had told her. "Did you stay at the clinic because you thought you'd wrecked my family?"

His shoulders stiffened. She thought he wouldn't answer, but he took another drink then said, "At first, maybe. You know I didn't like med school."

She nodded.

"I was almost grateful for an excuse to drop out. Then after…" He paused. "After you left and Julia was gone, I felt bad for your parents. They seemed shell-shocked by everything."

"That was a big club," Lainey murmured, hoping old bitterness didn't seep into her tone.

"The thing was, I liked working with the animals. I liked helping their owners. Taking care of them—it was good for me."

She thought about his strong hands holding Pita. Lainey had been so consumed by her own loss after the miscarriage, she'd barely considered Ethan's feelings. She'd assumed he felt relief at being released from his obligation to her. Now she could see that healing the animals had helped mend his scars.

He'd gone forward with his life, made a home and place in this community separate from the identity a small-town life thrust on its natives.

She'd moved forward, too, but kept the world at an arm's—or camera's—length away. Familiar resentment clogged her throat as she thought of the relationships she could have, the community and home she might have missed because of that.

"I'm happy for you." She busied herself tearing a strip of bacon into tiny pieces over her eggs.

Ethan's deep chuckle broke the quiet. "You made every meal your own particular combination of flavors. I'd forgotten that."

She shrugged but was surprised he'd ever noticed such a detail about her. "I like to get the perfect bite."

"Your photos are like that."

She thought about how she organized a shot—even on location—setting things up and putting in rocks or other natural props to improve the composition. She smiled. "It's kind of the same thing."

He watched her, his expression unreadable. "You haven't smiled much since you've been back."

Her face grew warm under his scrutiny. "What's with all the groceries?" She pointed to the bags on the counter, grateful for the distraction.

He took another bite and one big shoulder lifted. "You hardly had any food left."

"I live on cereal and Lean Cuisines when I'm at home."

"You loved to cook."

"I thought I *should* love to cook," she said. "I was *that* daughter."

"What daughter?"

A short curl fell into her face as she looked down at her plate. "You know. Julia was the pretty one. I had to…well… have other things to offer."

He sat back in his chair. "I didn't realize you grew up in the 1800s. Did you show potential boyfriends your teeth?"

There were no potential boyfriends, she thought. *Only you.* She stood and picked up both the empty plates, carrying them to the sink. "You don't know how it was to grow up with Julia."

"For what it's worth, I thought you were just as pretty."

Lainey snorted then slapped her hand over her mouth. "That is so not true," she said between her fingers. "No one knew I existed when she was around."

He pushed back from the table and walked over to her, gently prying her hand away from her face. His thumb traced light circles against the tender flesh on the inside of her wrist. A shiver rippled down Lainey's spine. "You were beautiful then and you're more beautiful now." He drew one finger along her bare neck.

She felt herself drift nearer to him, so close she could see each individual bristle of beard that shadowed his jaw.

Without warning, he turned away, grabbing a plastic bag from the counter. "I'll put this stuff away."

Lainey took a woozy step back, pushing her hip into the sink for balance. She bent to offer Pita the last bit of bacon and heard Ethan's mock growl behind her. "Busted," she said, ruffling the dog's ears. "Sorry, doc. Old habits die hard."

"Tell me about it," came his cryptic reply. He put away a box of Cheerios and turned to her. "What do you have planned today?"

Pita stretched and rolled onto her back to give Lainey better access to her soft belly. "I'll go see Mom with what's left of the morning, I guess. Pore over event plans later."

"I'm going fishing out at Stroud's Run. Want to come?"

Her hand stilled, and she felt the gentle rise and fall of Pita's chest under her fingers.

He'd asked the question lightly, as if they'd just be two old friends hanging out. Could that be possible? Suddenly, she didn't relish the long day that stretched in front of her.

"What time?"

He ran his fingers through his hair. "I've been meaning to come by the hospital. Why don't I meet you there around one?"

She nodded.

He took a step toward the door.

"Ethan?"

He glanced over his shoulder.

"Thanks again for breakfast." She wrapped her arms

around her chest, her thin T-shirt not enough protection against the heat of his gaze. "And for last night."

He tipped his head. "I'll see you later."

Chapter Nine

"What are you doing?"

Ethan adjusted the oversize vase of flowers he'd just purchased from the hospital gift shop. Not that he needed to see the woman talking to recognize the voice.

"I'm going to see your mom. What does it look like?" He would have continued down the hall, but Julia blocked his path, her round belly pointing at him like an arrow.

"I'm wondering," she said, a tinge of accusation in her voice, "if you're messing with my sister's head. Again."

Ethan's good mood from the morning dissolved as his temper flared. Because he thought they'd left the past behind and he and Julia were friends. Because he didn't want to admit that he worried about the same thing himself. "Mind your own business, Juls."

"My family is my business. We've had enough heartache to last a lifetime. There's a chance to start over this summer. I don't want anyone jeopardizing that. Even someone as well-intentioned as you, E." The saleslady from the gift shop leaned over the counter to eavesdrop.

He inclined his head. "Do you really want to do this here? You know how much people talk in this town."

A young woman with a baby walked into the gift shop, blocking them from view for a moment. He edged away until Julia grabbed his arm and hauled him across the hall.

She opened a door marked Stairwell and pulled him through.

The heavy fire door slammed shut with a bang. He took two steps away so her stomach wouldn't knock into him. "Jenny Baker," she whispered, "saw you kissing my sister in the Piggly Wiggly parking lot."

He leaned against the metal railing. "Jenny Baker should pay more attention to who her husband is kissing and not worry about other people."

Julia's delicate brows raised then she shook her head. "Don't try to distract me. What's going on with you and Lainey?"

"I don't know. I do know it's between Lainey and me."

"Like you said, this is Brevia. You know the drill." She said quietly, "Leave her alone, Ethan. She deserves someone better."

"How do you know—"

"Come on." She blew out a breath. "Everyone thinks you're the bee's knees, but I know the truth. You let the bus run right over Lainey. We both did." She put her palms on her hips. "I don't blame her for leaving. How else was she going to survive?"

"I didn't mean to hurt her," he argued. Talons of unease crept along his spine. He'd been messed up when he was with Lainey. He'd been messed up almost his entire life. Julia was right—she knew him better than most.

"Neither did I," she agreed. "We were all hurt. I wonder

what would have happened if I'd stayed in New York instead of coming back here that summer, if I hadn't been here the night you found out about the pregnancy."

"It wouldn't have mattered, Juls. You and I weren't going to get back together."

"We know that, but Lainey didn't ten years ago. She thought you were still in love with me. The point is we have a chance to make things better."

"Don't you think I want to help with that?"

"I don't know what you want. What I do know is that she may seem tough, but that girl—the one who worshiped you for so many years—she's still in there. I'm telling you straight up—don't hurt her again."

He wanted to fling the bouquet of flowers in the trash, leave the hospital for someplace where he could think. Where the Morgan women couldn't invade every cell of his body.

Instead, he straightened. "I understand your concern, Juls. I'm not going to hurt her. And right now I'm late to see Vera." He took the steps two at a time, not looking back.

Lainey stepped off the elevator and started toward her mother's room at the same time Ethan burst through the door leading from the stairwell.

He collided into her, the flowers he held tickling her face. His hand reached out to steady her.

"Hey." She smiled, wiping pollen off her nose with one finger.

A scowl drew down the sides of his wide mouth and his eyes were hard as he studied her. "Why are you here?" he practically barked.

She stepped away from him, wondering where the sweet, teasing man from earlier had gone. "Well…it's one o'clock. We're meeting."

"Right." He dropped his hand from her arm.

"Are you okay?" She'd seen that look in his eyes before,

remembered how he'd been after Julia had left all those years ago: angry, frustrated, lost. It tugged on her heart, on the quiet, deep place she'd thought she'd filled with work and travel.

"What can I do?" She didn't want to say the words, didn't want to care. With Ethan she couldn't help herself.

He searched her face for several heartbeats then trailed one finger down her forehead, between her brows, smoothing a crease she hadn't realized was there.

"I'm fine." He took her hand, laced his fingers in hers. "Let's go."

She let him lead her down the hall then drew her hand away when they reached her mother's room.

He frowned, a question in his dark gaze.

"Not here," she whispered and looked away. Before he could argue she stepped forward.

"Hi, there," she called out, making her voice purposely light.

Vera looked up from the book in her lap. Her gaze took in the two of them. Lainey knew this was a mistake, being here with him. Her mother didn't need another reason to judge her.

Vera only smiled. "For me?" she asked as Ethan stepped around Lainey.

"Who else?" He bent to hug her, placing the flowers on the bedside table.

She cupped his face. "How are the animals? Do they miss me?"

"We all miss you."

She patted his cheeks and drew him down to the side of the bed. "Tell me everything. Any new intakes? Who's been adopted?"

Lainey couldn't imagine with his busy schedule at the clinic that Ethan would've had the time or inclination to keep track of shelter business, but he patiently gave Vera a detailed status report.

Her mother listened, asking questions or making comments about certain animals. She handed Ethan a pad of paper and pen from her nightstand, dictating a mile-long list of instructions for him to relay to the shelter staff.

Since Lainey had been in town, Vera had made remarkable progress. Her speech was almost back to normal, although her right arm and leg still didn't function properly.

"Mom, you shouldn't worry about work," Lainey said, coming to stand at the foot of the bed. "The shelter is fine."

Vera turned as if Lainey had just bitten the head off a baby mouse. "Fine isn't good enough, Melanie," she huffed. "The shelter is your father's legacy. It matters."

Lainey struggled to control her breathing. "I know. Your health matters, too."

"I'm being released next week."

"That's great," Ethan said.

"Your leg," Lainey protested. "You can't walk."

"I'll get better at home. They'll give me exercises, and you can drive me to therapy appointments."

Lainey swallowed. "Of course."

"I need to get back to my life," her mother continued, leveling a look at her. "I'm no good to anyone in here."

Lainey's mouth twisted in annoyance. "Is this about the event? I'm not doing enough, right? You're pushing yourself because you don't think I can handle everything."

"It's *my* event, young lady. My reputation's on the line."

"Is it your friends? Do they have a problem with me?" Lainey didn't want to be so vulnerable in front of Ethan, but her fears and self-doubt tumbled forward like a landslide. "I'm doing my best, Mama. If you think you can do better in your condition, have at it. I have about a million places I'd rather be than stuck in Brevia for the summer."

"Do *not* take that tone with me, Melanie Lynne."

Lainey felt her composure begin to crumble. Her stomach burned with old resentment and pain. Then Ethan's large hand wrapped around her wrist.

"Show her the pictures," he said gently.

She glanced down at the envelope still clutched against her T-shirt. "I can't do this," she whispered miserably. "You show her."

Blocking her mother's view, he stroked his thumb against the racing pulse on the inside of her wrist. "Yes, you can."

Just as it had during that first meeting at the clinic, the look in his eyes bolstered her confidence and gave her comfort. She nodded and turned back to Vera.

"I'll be outside," he murmured and pushed open the door.

"What pictures?" her mother demanded.

"I took a few shots of the shelter animals for the website. I thought you'd want to see."

Her mother's chest rose and fell in deep breaths. She took the envelope wordlessly, fumbling with the metal clasp.

Lainey covered her mother's fingers with her own. "I'm sorry I lost my temper. I'm trying my best."

"I know." Vera pressed her head back against the pillow. "The shelter…the animals…they're all I have left of your father, Lainey. I need to be there." Her voice broke. "It's my only connection to him."

Lainey sank down to the edge of the bed. "I know how hard it was with Julia and me gone. If I hadn't left he wouldn't have been so sad and he might have stayed healthier." She wiped tears from her mother's cheeks.

Vera shook her head. "His heart was bad. What happened…his death…none of it was your fault. The heart attack was only a matter of time."

Something went still inside Lainey. She had carried the guilt of her dad's death like a traveling companion. It had gone with her to every destination, wrapped around her like a blanket under the remote skies in Africa, laid down beside her in a tent on a Costa Rican beach. Like the sorrow she felt for the baby she'd lost, she hadn't been able to outrun it or leave it behind.

"When I called…after…" Lainey's voice shook. "When I couldn't get here for the funeral…"

Her mother's face twisted. "I was overcome with grief. I was mad at your father for dying, mad that he hadn't gone to the doctor. I was angry with myself for not realizing how bad off he was. I was mad at you. I was mad at everyone. It wasn't your fault."

Sobs racked Lainey's body. Vera pulled her close and repeated, "It wasn't your fault."

"Oh, Mama. I miss him."

"Me, too, sweetie." Vera leaned back and wiped under her eyes. "I think he's with the baby," she said softly.

"What?" Goose bumps ran the length of Lainey's spine.

Her parents had been with her at the hospital when she'd miscarried, but they'd never discussed the baby she lost. They'd taken Lainey home, tucked her into bed and murmured platitudes about how "things happen for a reason."

Their relief at the outcome of her pregnancy had seemed palpable to Lainey. It had been a slap in the face, caused a rift in her relationship with them that had made leaving easier to bear.

"Your father was so sad for you," her mother continued, grabbing a tissue from the bedside table. "We both were. It makes me feel better to think he's with your baby."

Lainey was filled with a deep sense of…not exactly peace…yet something as freeing. A feeling of calm she hadn't known was missing from her life settled over her like a soft spring rain on the New Mexican mesas. Filling up the dry, barren desert until it once again bloomed with life.

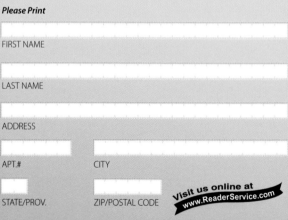

"Thank you," she mouthed to her mother, unable to produce the smallest sound. She wiped her nose and pulled the stack of pictures from the envelope. "Here," she said on a ragged breath.

As her mother looked down, a smile lit her face. She thumbed through the photos, taking several moments to study each one. Lainey walked to the window, gazing out as she worked to steady her heart.

When she turned, her mother watched her with a mix of curiosity and admiration. "These are lovely," she said, her voice trembling. "You've captured their personalities and a bit of their souls in these photos."

Lainey shrugged. "I thought it would help me to get to know them. Besides the website, I'm going to put together a brochure and flyer for the event."

"An excellent idea." Her mother hugged the stack of pictures to her chest. "These are more than photos, Lainey. They're portraits…true art. You have an amazing gift."

Lainey was so used to her mother's disapproval, jumping through hoop after hoop to measure up to Vera's high standards, she wasn't sure how to handle this tender moment. "Thank you," seemed ineffectual, still it was all she could manage.

"May I keep these?"

"Sure."

The door creaked open and Robert, the tattooed physical therapist, rolled a wheelchair into the room.

"Time for your workout," he announced as his gaze took in both Vera and Lainey's puffy, tearstained faces. He shot Lainey a glare before kneeling at Vera's side.

"What's going on?" he asked, taking Vera's tiny hand in his meaty one.

Lainey watched her mother smile at him. Holy cow, she

thought. This might be serious. A smile tugged at the corners of her mouth.

"She brought photos of my babies." Vera tilted the stack of pictures in his direction.

He leaned his shiny head forward. "Tell me about them." His total concentration was focused on Vera.

Lainey backed toward the door. "I'll talk to you later tonight, Mom."

Vera looked around Robert for a moment. "Love ya, honey," she called.

Lainey smiled. It was the first time her mother had said those words in over ten years. "Me, too, Mom."

She closed the door behind her and sagged against it, her eyes drifting shut. Her body felt like Jell-O, weak and almost weightless.

"Hey." Ethan stood in front of her, searching her face.

"I thought you'd gone." Her voice sounded far away in her own ears.

"I didn't know if you'd want to be alone."

She took another breath. "I'm good."

He looked surprised and relieved at the same time. "Do you still want to fish?"

"I do." She stopped when she realized the two words she'd uttered, steeped in meaning for them both.

He only smiled, his eyes crinkling at the corners. "Let's go."

The afternoon flew by in the blink of an eye for Ethan.

He'd packed a cooler with sandwiches, apple slices, chips and cream sodas. Sitting on the dock next to Lainey had made it feel like a gourmet feast. He couldn't remember the last time hanging out with a woman was so easy and exhilarating.

He quizzed her on her work, places she'd visited, adventures she'd had. When they'd been in college he'd been a huge jerk. In their short time together, he wasn't sure if he'd once asked her a question about herself and her interests.

He figured he had a lot to make up for. Maybe he'd deserved to be left at the altar. He didn't know what kind of husband he would have made—pretty bad if his own parents' marriage was any indication.

As the light began to fade behind the trees, Lainey stood and stretched. "I guess we should take off."

He pulled his line out of the water. "I didn't catch anything."

She scrunched up her face. "You didn't try too hard."

"Nope," he agreed.

"My dad always said fishing was one quarter what you caught and the rest an excuse for some peace and quiet."

"Your father was a smart man."

She lifted the blanket. "He would have been proud of what you've done with the clinic."

He shrugged. "I mainly try to stay out of your mom's way."

"I've spent most of my life with that goal." She looked out at the lake as a group of teenagers made their way down the far shore. "You know, I never came here in high school."

He heard a peal of laughter and the thump of rap music in the distance. "Never?"

"This is where the popular kids hung out—the girls with boyfriends. I spent my weekends in Annie Williams's basement, imagining what I'd do when a boy finally brought me here." Her smile was wistful. "It never happened."

"I thought everyone—"

She shook her head, taking a few steps toward the water.

"So who was the lucky guy in your plan?" he asked, trying to keep the conversation light. "Geez, not Tim I hope."

She turned, her eyes bright in the fading light. *"You don't know?* After all this time?" He heard her voice catch. "I'll give you a hint—the boy I dreamed about all through high school didn't know I existed."

Stunned, he could only stare at her. "Lainey, it wasn't like that. I knew you…"

She stood only a few feet away but might as well have been on the other side of the lake. He looked around wildly, desperate for a way to change the subject. His gaze caught on a flash of light through the trees.

"There's something I want to show you."

She glanced over her shoulder and pulled a face. "That's a bad line, even for you."

He grimaced but felt grateful she'd made a joke.

"Come on." He grabbed the cooler and fishing poles and headed toward the parking lot. After dropping the gear into the back of his pickup, he made his way to a small trail that snaked out of the woods.

He paused, waiting for Lainey to catch up as unrealistic anxiety skittered through him. *Pull it together, buddy. This is not a big deal.*

She studied him as she walked to the edge of the parking lot. "You're freaking me out. Should I be worried you're luring me into the deep, dark forest to exact some psycho plan for revenge?"

He flashed her a Jack Nicholson leer. "Do I look psycho?"

"Not reassuring," she muttered.

Grabbing her hand, he started up the path. "Trust me." Her palm felt smooth and warm against his. He liked touching her, like the feeling of connection and awareness that put each of his senses on high alert.

They walked in comfortable silence as shadows cast patterns along the forest floor. The trail was narrow, with thick green foliage creeping close on either side. He'd loved this forest since he was a boy, pedaling his bike miles from his home as often as he could. He'd lost himself in the peaceful stillness of the trees. It had been his sanctuary and escape from the chaos of his own house.

"Didn't your family own some land around the lake?"

"We're on it. I bought it from my granddad a few years ago. This is the place."

He watched her gaze lift, released the breath he hadn't realized he was holding as her jaw dropped.

"It's wonderful," she whispered.

"It's taken a few years. I work on it during weekends, and the clinic doesn't always leave time."

She walked toward the house. "You built this yourself?"

"Mainly," he answered, coming up behind her. He looked beyond her shoulder, trying to see the house with new eyes.

"Can I see inside?"

"The front door is unlocked."

"Show me."

He turned the handle and watched her step across the threshold. A feeling spread through him that this moment was exactly right. As if he'd been waiting to have her in his home. As if she belonged here.

His emotions stirred as she started up the stairs. Her fingers trailed along the wood rail, and his insides grew heavy in response. He followed her through the kitchen and out the French doors onto the deck, his favorite spot.

She leaned forward against the rail. "The view is incredible. You can see the whole lake from here."

"It is incredible." He traced his finger along the back of her neck. The need to touch her pulsed through his entire body.

Her eyes had turned stormy gray again, and in the dim light he could just make out the smattering of freckles across her nose.

"I like you here," he whispered and pressed his mouth to hers. He meant to keep the kiss light. But when he tasted the sweetness of her mouth, all the emotion swirling through him poured out.

He tried to tell her everything he couldn't say out loud. What this moment meant to him, having her in his home. That he was sorry it had taken him so long to realize how special she was.

He'd kissed more than a few women in his life; still nothing had felt like this. Like a piece of his soul was hanging out in the summer air.

When he lifted his head, her eyes were dazed. He knew he looked the same, but if she could see inside... He had to put some distance between them until he could pull his mask back into place.

"I need to check some work the electrician did this week. Are you okay out here for a few minutes?"

The question was clear in her eyes as she looked at him, but to his relief, she only nodded.

As Ethan disappeared inside, Lainey stared across the water at the kids on the other side. She'd dreamed of being part of a group like that when she was younger. A few times her senior year—once Ethan was safely away at college— she'd driven out here with her girlfriends, hiding at the edge of the woods as they'd watched the couples on a Saturday night.

A night like this, where the forest surrounding the lake hummed with the sound of insects and the wind off the water ruffled her hair. She'd imagined him bringing her to the lake, how it would feel to sit near a campfire with his arm around her shoulder.

She'd given up that fantasy years ago.

She wasn't the same lovesick girl who wore her heart on her sleeve. She'd spent too much time living in the shadow of her past mistakes. Now she longed to be whole. To feel like her life and the people in it belonged to her alone.

She rubbed her hands against her bare arms to calm a sudden flush of goose bumps.

"What are you thinking?"

The quiet rumble of Ethan's voice made her jump. She spun and tried to step away. He caught her and pulled her close.

"I can't—" she began then stopped when he covered her mouth with his. Without hesitation, she met his need with her own. She reached up and wrapped her arms around his neck, twining her fingers through his thick hair.

So much for her willpower.

With just a touch, Ethan made her forget all her pain. In its place burned a need years in the making. Suddenly, she was seventeen again and her dreams were coming true in the arms of the man she'd once loved with all her heart.

She dragged her mouth away from his. Digging her fingernails into the wood railing, she concentrated on breathing.

"I need to go home," she said, irritated that she sounded breathless.

His eyes were gentle yet dark as the shadowy woods as he stared at her, but he didn't argue. "If that's what you want."

Chapter Ten

"Are you sure you don't want some place not so busy?" Ethan asked as he angled into a parking spot. "And with better food." A crowd of people spilled onto Carl's outside patio.

"Everyone but you loves Carl's," Steph said as she climbed out of the truck. She'd badgered him into taking her to lunch. Truth be told, he was glad to get a break from his own company. "Best onion rings this side of the Smoky Mountains."

"My arteries are clogging already," he answered. A bead of sweat rolled down between his shoulder blades. It wasn't unbearably hot for August and a light breeze tickled the back of his neck. Why was he suddenly roasting?

Steph didn't notice. "I'll get a table." She took off down the street as he locked the truck. He'd just finished putting change in the meter when she reappeared at his side.

"It's too crowded," she said quickly. "Let's go someplace else."

One last quarter dropped in the slot. "We're here now. Carl

will find us a table. Or we can sit at the bar." He turned to look at the restaurant's entrance. Steph jumped in front of him.

"It's not worth it," she insisted. "We can pick up Chinese and eat at the clinic."

"I put a buck fifty in the meter. What's your problem?" He ducked around her and stopped in his tracks.

A couple was being shown to a table on the enclosed patio in front of the restaurant. Ethan's mouth went dry as Tim Reynolds placed a hand on Lainey's back and leaned close to whisper something in her ear. She laughed and slipped into her chair, gazing at Tim with her sweet, open smile. Her sleeveless black dress hugged every curve on her body—it was the kind of dress a woman wore on a real date.

Anger bubbled up inside him as he took off for the restaurant. Steph hung on to his arm with all her strength.

"Whoa, there, killer," she said.

"Do you see how he's looking at her?" Ethan could hardly see straight for the possessive rage he suddenly felt. "How he touched her?"

"Um, Conan, before you drag her off to your cave, think about how it's going to make you look."

"I don't give a…" He stopped and took a breath. "Fine," he muttered, disgusted that he couldn't put Tim in his place. "We'll play it your way."

"My way? I don't have a way," she protested, tripping in her attempt to keep up with him.

They were almost to the restaurant when Tim noticed them. He leaned forward and spoke quickly to Lainey. She turned as Ethan and Steph got to the table.

"What are you doing here with him?" Ethan asked, his plan to play it cool totally forgotten. Out of the corner of his eye, he saw Tim stand.

"Dude, we're on a date," Tim said. "Do you mind?"

Lainey's chin tilted. "Tim and I need to discuss possible articles to promote the adoption fair. It's a working lunch."

He tried not to let her scent invade his senses. "You print a few pictures of furry animals on the front page. You need a black dress for that?"

Lainey's eyes narrowed. "You're way out of line."

Patrons at other tables looked over, whispering to each other. He wanted everyone in the restaurant to go away, to leave him alone with Lainey. If it was just the two of them, maybe he could calm down—figure out how to make things right. After she'd gone home last night, Ethan had spent hours awake wondering how to show her she still meant so much to him. In his heart, they belonged together. Something about Tim with Lainey wound around his gut and wouldn't let go.

He tried to rein in his fury. "I can pull up stories from previous events—families that have kept in touch about their adoptive pets," he said quietly.

Her expression turned confused, but she smiled slightly. "That would be great."

He couldn't ignore the feelings that seeing her with Tim conjured, but it didn't help either of them to cover his fear with anger. Any man would count his lucky stars to have her on his arm.

What if she realized how much better she could do than him? What if she didn't give him another chance?

He wanted to reach forward and touch the soft strands of her hair. Her dress scooped in front, revealing just a trace of her pale, freckled skin. He noticed a faint blush of pink work its way up from her chest to her cheeks. He couldn't tear his eyes away.

Tim cleared his throat. His trance broken, Ethan glanced at the other man. He wanted to rip Tim's throat out, and it looked like the feeling was mutual.

Steph grabbed his arm. "We should get a table," she said, yanking on him.

He looked at Lainey. Her lashes fluttered down over her green eyes, veiling their expression. It amazed him that her lashes didn't tangle when she blinked, that's how long they were. She wouldn't meet his eyes, but her lips pressed together in a thin line.

Ethan couldn't pretend seeing her with Tim didn't make him want to go ballistic, and he had no intention of sitting down with Steph to watch the whole scene. "I lost my appetite."

He turned on his heel and stalked down the street, not particularly caring if Steph followed. But she scrambled into the seat next to him as he threw the truck in Reverse and slammed on the gas, almost hitting another car as he pulled out.

After a few minutes, Steph spoke. "Ethan, this isn't the Daytona 500. Could you slow down?"

He looked at the speedometer then pulled into the parking lot of Burger Bucket, Brevia's version of fast food.

"I'm sorry, but did you see that?" he yelled. "She was on a date. With Tim Reynolds."

Steph made a face. "I'm not sure what you saw, but they were having lunch. And talking business, for heaven's sake."

"So what? You saw how he looked at her."

"Yeah, well, she looked really good."

"More than good. She looked amazing." He ran his hands through his hair. "What was she doing with *him?*"

"At the risk of repeating myself, they were *eating lunch.* Friends do that. She's been friends with him for years."

He sighed. "The whole scene threw me. The Lainey I knew didn't wear tight dresses and go on lunch dates."

"Maybe you don't know her that well," Steph suggested.

Ethan rested his head against the seat back and closed his

eyes. A picture of Lainey tossing her hair and smiling at another man filled his mind.

"That's obvious." He opened his eyes to clear the scene. "Am I such a first-rate fool?"

Steph smiled. "Is that a rhetorical question?"

"Hell, yes," he answered.

Lainey swallowed against the anger that squeezed her throat as Tim swung his car into the parking space next to her Land Cruiser. He'd met her in front of the newspaper office and driven the short distance to Carl's.

"Are you okay?" he asked, turning to face her.

She tried to smile but couldn't quite coax her mouth into moving. "Sure," she said.

"He's acting like a jerk," Tim said. "He never did deserve you."

"You don't have to say that. I know you two are friends."

He shook his head. "I don't care about Ethan. You're the one who's important to me. Do you understand?"

"I guess." Something about the gleam in Tim's eyes made the hair on her bare arms stand on end. His gaze strayed to her chest. She hadn't purposely worn a dress that could be misconstrued as a come-on. The way he looked at her said she'd made a mistake.

"He can't make you happy—will never give what you want."

Her shoulders stiffened. "What I want is to make the adoption event a success and get back to my life."

"Trust me. We're on the same page."

She wanted to trust Tim, needed people in her corner as she worked on the event. She didn't remember Tim's behavior being so suffocating in high school. Lunch had been uncomfortable, and while she'd blamed that on Ethan's interruption, now she wasn't sure. "Thanks again for lunch. I'll call you next week to confirm the run dates." She reached for the door handle.

"Do you think there's a chance for us, Lainey?"

Her head whipped around. "Excuse me?"

"I'm sorry. I shouldn't have blurted that out." His hands clenched and unclenched in an unnatural rhythm. "You must know how I feel about you. How I've always felt."

"We're old friends, Tim." She cringed at the pain that flashed in his eyes. If there was one thing Lainey knew a lot about, it was unrequited love. "That's all. I don't want to hurt you but…"

"It could be more," he interrupted. "If Ethan wasn't in the picture, if you could forget about him…" He grabbed her wrist and leaned in close. "I don't want to see *you* hurt again." His lips thinned. "He doesn't care about you, Lainey. He never did."

She met his gaze steadily, unwilling to admit how his words spoke to her deepest fears. "Let go of me. Now."

He released her wrist, and she climbed out of the car quickly, slamming the door. He rolled down the passenger window. "I could make you happy, Lainey. I want what's best for you," he said, his tone placating.

"Assign someone else to work with me on publicity, Tim. You need to back off." She turned on her heel and stalked toward her car.

She spent the rest of the afternoon busy with plans for the adoption fair and preparations for her mother to come home, trying to shake off the strange feeling from lunch.

After uploading the pictures she'd taken of the animals to the shelter's website, she'd printed posters to hang in local businesses. To her surprise, once she'd delivered a couple to Carl's Diner and Piggly Wiggly, other merchants called to request them over the next few days. It wasn't as bad as she'd thought to visit with people she'd known since child-hood. Only a couple dropped not-so-subtle digs about Ethan.

The more time she spent with the shelter staff and the animals, the more dedicated she became to making the adoption fair the best this town had ever seen. Not to make amends for old wrongs but because the animals deserved it. So many pets needed good homes. Her heart broke each time a new dog, cat, or even guinea pig was processed into the shelter.

She brought Pita with her to work each morning and found it hard to imagine her life without the lovable mutt that spent most of her time curled in a ball at Lainey's feet.

A few days ago a tiny black Lab pup had been found wandering across the two-lane highway leading out of town. He had no collar and hadn't been claimed yet.

As if she could sense the puppy's need, Pita had followed the wee pup back and forth between the shelter and the clinic. The pup had sniffed and nipped playfully at the older dog, whining incessantly when they were separated. It had gotten so bad that they'd finally moved the puppy's cage into Lainey's office.

Still it wasn't enough. The puppy cried and Pita paced until Lainey opened the cage door. Pita climbed onto her dog bed and the puppy pressed against her belly. Now they were a group of three, and Lainey wondered how her no-strings-attached life had become complicated so quickly.

She glanced at her watch, needing to meet Julia for their first birthing class in twenty minutes. She stood and stretched—tired from hours of work and updating the shelter's website.

As she opened the door of her office, peals of laughter and a few barks rang out from the rear of the building.

She stepped out the back door as Steph's twins, the puppy, and Pita ran by. Joey, Steph's older son, waved from where he stood with Ethan and his mom, watching the game of chase.

Sam, one of the six-year-old twins, stopped when he saw her. "Lainey, your dog's a nut ball," he called as the puppy caught up to him. Pita ran circles around the two, barking happily before joining the pup in covering Sam's face with slobbery licks.

Sam squealed as he rolled on the ground. "Help, help," he yelled, "they're killing me with stinky kisses."

The boy looked happy enough, but kids in distress made Lainey nervous. "Pita, come here." She hurried off the steps. Pita trotted over, and Lainey wrapped her fingers around the dog's collar. "You're not a puppy. You have to be gentle."

"Don't worry," Steph said. "I'm hoping they'll wear him out enough to fall asleep before ten."

Lainey eased her grip on Pita's collar. The dog nuzzled her palm. "He yelled 'help,'" she said weakly, realizing it had been in jest.

Ethan grabbed a football off the ground. "Joey, go long," he called, running toward the center of the yard. "Keep away from the twin terrors."

The boys screamed in delight and gave chase, dogs trailing at their heels.

"I hope a family with young kids adopts her." Lainey made her voice purposely cheerful.

"Puppies are a lot of work but worth it."

Lainey slanted a glance at her friend. "I meant Pita."

Steph turned. "Pita's your dog."

"Not really." Lainey shrugged even as an invisible vice clamped around her midsection. "I can't keep her forever. I wasn't meant to…my job…I travel too much to have a pet."

"And you think you can let her go?" Steph asked, her voice quiet.

"I have to." Lainey blinked several times. "It's what's best."

"Uh-huh," was Steph's only answer. "Go get him, Sam," she cheered when Ethan stole the ball. "Kick his butt."

The six-year-old let out a rebel yell and charged after Ethan. Ethan slowed as the puppy nipped at his ankles and Sam launched onto his back. Ethan went down with an *oof* as Sam, his brother David and then Joey climbed on him.

"Should we rescue someone?" Lainey asked.

Steph shook her head. "Ethan's used to it. The boys are here a lot after school. He always makes time for them." She sighed. "My no-good ex-husband could take lessons."

A thought pricked at the back of her mind. "Joey's eight now?"

Steph nodded. "Starting third grade in a few weeks."

Ten years ago...

She clutched her hands to her stomach and turned away. Her baby would have been nine, only a year older than Joey. She thought about the child she'd lost sometimes, not as often as she used to, but always in terms of small babies. Not a half-grown child with a personality and needs. Hugs and kisses, scraped knees she'd never tend, hurt feelings she wouldn't get to soothe, late-night cuddles she'd never enjoy.

Her vision clouded. Pita was suddenly at her side, nudging against her bare leg.

"Lainey?" Steph's voice was soft next to her ear.

Lainey waved a hand in front of her face. "Sorry. Bug in my eye."

She felt Ethan's eyes on her and met his gaze across the backyard. He stood with David and Sam hanging off him, the muscles in his arms bulging. The deep understanding in his gaze told her he knew exactly what she was thinking.

She made her smile purposely bright. "Don't let him up so easy," she called.

"Hey!" Ethan protested.

The boys gave simultaneous war whoops. Legs and arms went flying.

"I'm okay." She glanced at Steph. "I promise."

Ethan staggered over, the boys holding tight to his legs. "Have mercy on me." The boys giggled.

"Joey. Samuel. David. Off." Steph's voice was gentle but firm.

All three let go, dropping to the ground as the puppy scrambled between them.

"How'd you do that?"

"I read your mom's book." Steph grinned. "Same principle for boys as puppies."

"Chip has puppy breath," Joey whined.

"Chip?" Ethan asked.

David flashed a sheepish smile. "We named him to match Pita."

"Pita. Chip. Cute." Ethan ruffled David's curly blond hair.

The puppy gave Sam a small nip then scampered over to Pita.

"Sorry, Chip." Lainey lifted the fluffy pup, nuzzling its downy fur against her chin. "I need to drop your friend Pita at home." She glanced at her watch. "Yikes. I'm really late."

Ethan scooped Chip out of her arms. "You can leave Pita here until you're finished." His eyes searched hers. "I'm sorry about earlier," he said softly. "I was way out of line."

She nodded. "It wasn't a date."

"Even if it was…" His eyes narrowed. "That's not where you're going now is it? To see Tim? I mean, it's cool, I just…"

"I have a Lamaze class."

Steph's loud snort of laughter drowned out Ethan's response. "You know it's *wrong* on so many levels that you're her birth coach."

"Yeah, well…" There was an awkward silence as Ethan stared at Lainey, a scowl darkening his face and making him all the more gorgeous. She wondered what he was thinking, if the family he'd wanted so badly still crossed his mind.

"I'll be back around seven-thirty."

He nodded. "We'll be here."

She gave Steph a quick hug and high-fived Joey, Sam and David. Despite hitting almost every red light on the way, she was only about fifteen minutes late.

With an apologetic wave, Lainey hurried to where Julia sat by herself at the far end of the room.

"You're late."

"I'm here now." Lainey sank down on the carpet.

"Look at all these happy couples," Julia mumbled as the instructor began her lecture again. "I feel like a complete loser."

"Jeff's an idiot if he's willing to miss this."

Julia flashed a small smile. "Thanks."

Lainey realized she may have spoken too soon as the teacher, Nancy, instructed the coaches to sit behind their partners, legs open. Julia leaned back against Lainey.

"Feel your breath," Nancy told the coaches. "Let the rise and fall of your chest guide the mother in her breathing."

Simple enough, except as soon as Lainey put her hands on either side of Julia's hard belly, she felt a firm kick.

"Holy cow," she said on a gulp.

She moved her hands to a different spot and was rewarded with an even stronger thump, thump, thump. She glanced over Julia's shoulder and saw rippling under the thin yellow T-shirt Julia wore.

She yanked her hands away. "Who's in there—the kid from *The Exorcist?*"

Julia sighed, pushing Lainey's hands back. "Pay attention."

Lainey tried to focus on Nancy's words but continued to be distracted by the movement under her fingers. In her line of work, it was relatively easy to steer clear of pregnant women. Animals were a different matter, but Lainey had never found herself staring wistfully at a tiger's distended stomach.

With the life growing inside her sister literally pulsing

under her hands, Lainey felt a black hole of despair begin to tear open in her own barren womb.

"What is going *on?*" Julia sat up and glanced back.

Lainey let her eyes drift shut for a moment. "Nothing. I'm trying to listen."

"*I'm* trying to match my breathing to yours, which is hard when you're hyperventilating."

"I'm not…" Lainey felt her chest heave up and down. She forced herself to take a deep breath. "I don't know if I can do this," she whispered.

"Please." Julia's chin hitched up a notch. "You're all I've got."

Despite her pounding heart and the sweat beading on her brow, Lainey kept her hands on her sister's stomach. "Turn around then."

Julia swallowed and leaned back.

By the grace of God, the baby remained still for the rest of the class. Lainey concentrated on Julia, on how they would get through her eventual labor.

Once Lainey had her emotions under control, the class wasn't bad. She liked feeling connected. For so long, she'd kept her emotional distance from anyone who wanted to get close. She used her work to build walls around her shattered heart. But even after her heart had healed, she'd still been stuck in her lonely fortress.

They walked to the rec center parking lot after class. It was late, but voices of families enjoying the outdoor pool during the last weeks of summer drifted over the fence.

"So I'm an official coach." Lainey hefted Julia's bag of comfort items to one shoulder and scanned the parking lot.

"Only three more classes to go."

"Three more?"

"Didn't I mention," Julia asked, looking guilty, "that this is a month-long session?"

"No big deal. I'm here anyway." She gave Julia a quick hug.

When Lainey would have let go, Julia held tight. "I'm glad you came back."

Lainey felt her heart expand and pushed away, needing distance. "Where's your car?"

"It had a dead battery. My neighbor gave me a lift." She reached for her bag. "I'll call her to come get me."

"I can take you home."

Julia nodded. "Thanks."

When they got to the SUV, Lainey moved her camera equipment to the backseat.

"Maybe I could take a few shots of you," she suggested. As soon as the words were out, she gave herself a mental head thump. Not smart—focusing her camera on Julia's ripe stomach.

"That would be cool." Julia's tone was wry. "Unless you're asking so you can have proof of how fat I got."

"Give me a break. Eight months pregnant and most women would kill for your hips."

Julia rested her head on the back of the seat. "Jeff liked to remind me that my looks would fade and then I'd have nothing to offer. No brains, no talent, no real skills."

"He did a number on you."

"Maybe. It was an easy line to buy because I already believed it." Julia sighed. "Lord, I was jealous of you growing up."

Lainey glanced over as she pulled out of the parking lot. "That's funny, Juls."

"I'm serious. You were perfect—good grades, honor society, nice friends. You never gave Mom and Dad any trouble."

Lainey snorted. "Until your ex-boyfriend got me pregnant."

Julia dismissed that with a wave of her hand. "Then you left and became this world-famous photographer."

"I'm not exactly famous."

"Whatever. You're in *National Geographic*. People have those things on their shelves forever. My work lasts until someone's next bang trim."

"It's not the same thing," Lainey argued.

"That's my point. You have a legacy. I have a plastic crown from prom."

Emotion bubbled inside Lainey. "You're about to have a baby. That trumps a few magazine layouts in the legacy competition."

"You're only twenty-eight," Julia said. "Not exactly old-maid time. You'll meet someone, try again."

"I won't."

"Who knows," Julia continued as if Lainey hadn't spoken, "I've seen the way Ethan looks at you."

"No." Lainey wrenched the steering wheel, and the Land Cruiser skidded into the gravel on the side of the road.

"What the—" Julia cried as dust flew around them.

Lainey slammed her foot on the brake and threw the car into Park. Her fingers gripped the wheel, white-knuckled, and she kept her gaze trained on the horizon. "I *will not* have a baby," she said, enunciating each word.

"You can't know…"

Lainey spun in her seat, unlatching her seat belt as it cut across her neck. "I do know," she screamed. "I won't have a baby. I can't, Julia."

She expected tears to come but only felt a white-hot burning in her throat.

"I don't understand."

Lainey swallowed to ease her pain. She looked out the window past Julia's shoulder. "There were complications from the miscarriage." She shook her head. "I can't have a baby," she repeated.

Julia's cool fingers wrapped around Lainey's fisted ones.

"I'm sorry," her sister whispered. "What did Ethan say? Is that why you left?"

Lainey pulled her hands into her lap. "I didn't tell Ethan right away. I was too devastated. If he'd looked at me with pity I'm not sure I could have stood it."

"When did you tell him?"

"I left a note at the church. I know it was wrong and cowardly, but I was half crazed at that point. Looking at myself in the wedding dress, I couldn't go through with it. I was wearing white and all I could see was red—the blood—there was so much blood. I knew we wouldn't have stood a chance if he didn't know the whole truth. But I *could not* face him."

"So you ran off?"

"I asked him to meet me at the hotel in Charlotte where we were going for our honeymoon if he could be with me knowing everything."

"And?" Julia prompted.

"He never showed."

A look of disbelief crossed Julia's face. "That doesn't sound like Ethan."

Lainey shook her head. "I'd worshipped him for so long. I doubt we ever had a chance. I tried anything I could to make him happy so he'd forget I wasn't you."

"Did you try being yourself?"

"Yeah, right." Lainey pushed her hair behind her ears. "Mom made it very clear that being me didn't hold a candle to being you. Why would Ethan be any different?"

"You should talk to him."

"No way." Lainey shifted into gear. Her stomach clenched. "I have a life of my own now. What happened ten years ago is old news. I don't *want* another chance."

"Are you sure?"

She thought about how it felt to be with Ethan. Just one smile from him made her whole body light up. But she had to protect her heart. She was incomplete, and there was nothing in Brevia that could fill her.

She pulled up in front of the duplex Julia rented near downtown. "It's the only way."

Chapter Eleven

Ethan heard an engine turn off as an unfamiliar tremor of excitement shivered across his chest.

Pita stood and paced circles near the front door, the fur on her back standing on end. Ethan wondered at her reaction. "It's okay, girl."

A knock sounded and the dog growled softly. Ethan wanted to do the same as he identified the man on the other side.

"Hey, son." Ray Daniels took a drag on his cigarette, dropped it on the makeshift porch and ground it under the toe of his dirty sneaker. "How 'bout a hug for your old man?"

Ethan shifted to completely fill the doorframe. The dim evening light threw his father's face into shadow. Pita poked her head around his knee and growled low in her throat. Good instincts, that dog. "What are you doing here?"

Ray glanced at Pita. "Pick up *another* stray, didya? When are you going to stop with the animals?"

"What do you want, Dad?"

A path of deep and sunburned lines wove a pattern around Ray's eyes. It had been two years since his last unannounced visit. He'd aged badly since then. Late nights, forty years of smokes and a taste for Wild Turkey would do that to a man.

"Are you going to invite your old man in, or is your trailer too good for me?"

Ethan stepped back. "I move into the lake house in a couple of weeks," he said through clenched teeth.

"Got a beer?" Ray asked, opening the refrigerator door. "The photos Lainey Morgan took of the shelter mutts were on the front page down in Charleston." Ray used the corner of the counter to pop the top on a bottle of beer. "I can't believe that little tramp has the nerve to show up here after what she did."

"You should stop talking." Ethan clenched his fists to keep from wrapping them around his father's scrawny throat. "She has every right to be here. Vera had a stroke, Dad. Lainey's been helping her."

Ray hitched one hip onto the counter. "Didn't you learn anything from your mama running out on us? The difficult ones aren't worth the trouble. Are you gonna let Lainey mess with your life all over again? You could've been a real M.D., not some backwoods pet vet."

"I like my job."

"Is she that good between the sheets that you'd go running back? Her sister I can understand. I might have tapped that blonde goddess in my day but Lainey—"

Ethan crossed the space in two steps. He grabbed the bottle as Ray lifted it and threw it into the sink with a clatter. "Get out. Now."

Ray lifted his hands, palms out. "I'm between jobs. Thought I might stick around for the big shindig."

"I don't want you anywhere near here."

"I only want what's best for you, son. And Lainey ain't it.

Trust me, I know women, and that one's gonna mess you up bad," he said with a smirk. "I'm staying with your uncle Tony. He's got room since wife number three took off." Ray walked to the door. "Think about what I said and I'll see you around."

Ethan didn't turn as the door slammed shut. His father in town was a complication he didn't need. He'd almost steadied his breathing when his cell phone buzzed from the coffee table. He picked it up, listened for a few moments and muttered a curse.

"I'll be right there."

Grabbing his keys, he hollered over his shoulder, "Let's go, Pita."

It was the longest ten-minute drive of his life. Lainey had been crying so hard he couldn't understand much of what she'd said, only that she needed help. His imagination went wild imagining what might have happened. He saw her car on the side of the two-lane highway, a shadow in the haze of early evening with the hazards blinking like a lighthouse beacon. He barely pulled to a stop before jumping out of the truck.

The driver's side door swung open, the interior light making her hair glow like a patch of sunlight. "I'm here."

As her head lifted, a shadow of frustration crossed her face. "That was quick." She flashed a smile. "How fast were you driving?"

"Are you okay? Were you hurt?" He scanned her body expecting injuries, took her face between his palms. "Can you focus on me?"

"Unfortunately, yes," she whispered as she shrugged out of his grasp. A minivan rumbled past, its engine drowning out her next words. "I blew a tire," she said when the quiet settled again. "Not exactly an emergency."

"It sure as hell sounded like an emergency."

"I had a bad day. A flat tire was the last thing I needed. I overreacted. Sorry." She narrowed her eyes. "Stop looking at me like that."

"Are you going to tell me what happened?"

"I went over a nail or something. I don't know."

"I mean tonight. With Julia."

Her teeth tugged on her bottom lip. "Nothing. We went to class." She turned to the glove compartment. "I have the owner's manual in here. It tells you how to change a tire."

"I know how to put on a spare," he snapped. He didn't need another dose of attitude after his father's visit.

His life may not have been the one he'd planned, but it worked. Ethan didn't need to think too deeply to get through things. He could leave his feelings and his pain buried, just where he liked them. Being near Lainey made him think about too much that he didn't want to deal with—his past, his shortcomings, his empty life.

He'd thought he could make this summer easier for her and it would right all his wrongs. Assuming he could keep his heart out of the mix was stupid.

His gaze settled on her trembling fingers as she fumbled with the latch for the glove compartment then shifted to her face where color crept into her cheeks, her jaw tight with obvious frustration. He couldn't stand to see her like this.

"Come on," he said and reached in front of her to take the keys out of the ignition. "It's almost dark. I'll take you home and change the tire in the morning."

"Pita—"

He straightened, keys in hand. "Is in the truck. It's not safe to let her out here." As if on cue, a round of muted barking split the night air.

Her eyes squeezed shut for a moment. "I need to get my camera out of the back." Gravel crunched as she climbed out next to him. He reached forward and traced his finger along her jawline, hoping to relieve some of her tension. A shiver ran down her body, and the air surrounding them grew heavy with emotions he thought he'd left safely behind in his youth.

For now he stepped away. He shut the door and near darkness swallowed them. "Get your stuff. I'll be in the truck."

Lainey stood on the side of the road for several seconds before making her way to the back of the SUV. She felt open, exposed and once again attached to Brevia. She'd stayed away from connections that could lead to heartache since she'd left a decade ago. It wasn't the best life, but she knew it and could manage the consequences of her decisions. What she couldn't handle were her mother's expectations, her sister depending on her and the man waiting to drive her home. Even a dog seemed like too much of a burden right now.

She stalked toward the truck and flung her equipment into the backseat. Pita waited with enthusiastic tail wagging. The urge to wrap her arms around the dog's fluffy neck flashed.

No.

She didn't need anyone or anything in Brevia. "Pita, down." Her voice reflected her temper, and guilt immediately coursed through her as the dog flattened itself against the backseat.

Lainey heaved a sigh as she climbed in next to Ethan.

"What's the matter?"

She made a show of digging through her purse. "I'm tired and ready to be home."

His mouth thinned as he watched her. Maybe he wondered if she meant her home in New Mexico or her mother's house. Right now, she didn't know.

He eased the truck on to the highway. Grateful for the silence, she studied the occasional lights of farmhouses out the window and the pale white line at the side of the road. Soon her attention refocused on the man next to her and the dog's soft snoring from the backseat. The companionable stillness only heightened her nerves.

They were at the house in a few minutes. A light glowed in one of the upstairs windows. For a split second, she wished her mother was waiting then cursed her own weakness.

As soon as the truck stopped, Lainey scrambled out, the dog at her heels. "Thanks for the ride," she called over her shoulder, not daring to look back. She needed space. Ethan's door slammed shut as she fumbled with her keys and Pita danced around her legs.

Without switching on the light, she walked into the kitchen. She rested her hands on the table and counted backward from ten, pictured her mother, sang the ABC's in her head, anything to forget the way her body ached.

She didn't move, didn't speak. Only a minute more and she'd be back to normal.

Until he touched her.

Only the brush of fingers against the top of her arm. She waited for him to pull her to him. He continued to trace a light pattern across her skin. Nothing more.

"What are you doing?"

"Trying not to pressure you. To give you space." He paused. "Trying to be the man you want me to be."

"Ethan, I don't know..."

He pulled his hand away. "What do you want, Lainey?" he whispered. "Do you want me to go? I will. You need time? I'll give it to you. But tell me—"

She whirled and pressed her mouth hard against his. She couldn't say what she wanted, but at this moment she knew to the depths of her soul she needed his kiss.

Maybe it was wrong.

Of course it was wrong.

She wasn't nineteen anymore with youth as an excuse to be swept away in the moment. She knew better. Life wasn't a fairy tale, and even loving someone with your whole self didn't guarantee a happy ending.

She didn't care about how this ended. Didn't care if being with him ripped open her heart yet again.

She needed him so much it made her body shudder.

Before she knew it, he'd lifted her shirt over her head. She tried to turn to him, but he pulled her back against his chest. Somehow, he'd pulled off his shirt, too, and his chest hair tickled her bare back.

He lifted one bra strap slowly, kissing her shoulder, then let it fall down around her elbow. She clutched at his arm as his hand cupped her breast. He tilted her face to his and kissed her deeply, catching her moan in his mouth.

"My legs," she breathed. "I don't think…"

He laughed low as he scooped her into his arms.

He carried her up the stairs, his mouth never leaving hers. A shaft of moonlight sifted through the bedroom curtains as he laid her down against the pillows. She watched him undress, as always overwhelmed by his pure physical perfection.

She glanced down at her faded beige bra. "I'm sorry. I would have worn something…you know, fancy, if I'd thought…"

Ethan bent his head and dropped a line of kisses from her rib cage to where the top of her jeans skimmed her hips.

"Do you remember the first time we made love?" he asked.

"Uh-huh." She licked her lips, finding it hard to concentrate as he ran his tongue across her belly button.

"You were wearing a white bra." As he spoke, he pulled the jeans down around her hips. "It had one small bow right in the middle." His eyes darkened to the color of melted chocolate. "Kind of like the one you're wearing now."

If her mind hadn't been so clouded by desire, Lainey might have laughed. She'd been buying the same style of bras for as long as she could remember. At least ten years, apparently.

He tossed her jeans off the bed and skimmed his hands up her legs from her ankles, finally coming to rest on her hips.

His fingers grazed under the waistband of her panties then pulled her down until she was flat on the mattress, gazing into his dark eyes.

"I have never been so turned on by a woman as I was that night."

She closed her eyes and gave into the pleasure of feeling his body above hers. His lips didn't quite touch her, his breath cool as it blew against her hot skin.

"Until now," he whispered.

Her eyes flew open. "Really?"

He smoothed back the hair from her face, cradling her head in his hands with such tenderness tears pricked the back of her eyes.

"Yes, Lainey. Really."

It seemed impossible, but she knew he was telling the truth. Never once could she have imagined he wanted her that much. His desire was liberating.

Lainey gave herself over to her body. She didn't think, didn't analyze. No second-guessing or worrying about how she didn't measure up. They rolled together, a tangle of arms and legs until they finally melded into one.

Later—much later—he pulled her close, settling her back against his chest as he wrapped around her, cocooning her in his warmth. She fell asleep that way and when she woke, his arm was still snug across her chest.

The next several days kept Lainey busy. In addition to the animals at All Creatures Great and Small, adoptable pets would be brought in from shelters as far away as Atlanta. She needed to make sure a plan for housing the animals was worked out in advance. Without Vera, Ethan became the resident expert on animal behavior, so he decided on the best arrangement.

He also made dozens of phone calls to local and regional

businesses soliciting donations for raffle prizes and silent auction items. She'd tried not to be alone with him since the night they'd slept together, her only hope for self-preservation, but couldn't stop her body from craving his touch.

It felt like he could read her mind. He didn't try to kiss or hold her again, but when no one was looking she caught him staring at her, a wolfish smile curving his lips. Every look he gave her was like nonphysical foreplay—as if there could be such a thing.

Lainey took to walking around the shelter several times each hour just to catch her breath. *Get a grip,* she told herself. *It was sex. You've had sex before.* Maybe not for a while and never so good it left a glow three days later.

But still just sex. Nothing more. Nothing at all.

This was day number four, and she felt like an addict itching for a fix. Which may have explained why she was on her fifth lap around the building.

"You're wearing a path in the grass."

Ethan's voice snapped her out of her thoughts. He stood a few feet to her side on the lawn between the shelter and clinic buildings.

She pressed her hand to her heart. "You shouldn't sneak up on a person like that."

"I've been watching you circle the property for ten minutes. I'm starting to get dizzy."

"I needed a break. I think better when I'm moving."

He shifted his weight to one foot and adjusted the ball cap on his head. "What are you thinking about?" he asked, his voice laced with meaning.

She stomped one foot. "You're an egomaniac. For your information, you are not one bit on my mind."

His smile told her he knew exactly what she was thinking. "I have a couple of charts to finish. Do you want to grab dinner later?"

"I'm not hungry." Her stomach growled.

"Thirty minutes?"

"We shouldn't be seen together."

His smile vanished. "Why?"

"People will talk."

He moved in on her so quickly she didn't have time to dart away. "Darlin'," he said, his face inches from hers, "tongues have been wagging about us since you drove over the county line. Why do you care?"

"No one wants me messing with you."

"Are you messing with me?"

She stepped to the side, needing breathing space. "You know my deal. What I can and can't give."

"It's dinner." He flashed a coaxing smile. "What's the worst that could happen? What are you so afraid of?"

"Fine," she huffed, shaking her head. "But as friends."

"With amazing benefits?" he asked, winking.

She picked up a ratty tennis ball from the yard and shook it at his head. "Don't try anything funny. I mean it."

In exactly thirty-one minutes he came to the makeshift studio she'd set up in one of the shelter's empty offices.

He'd showered and changed into dark jeans and a pale green button-down shirt. His smile flashed model white against a tanned face. She pulled her hair from its loose bun.

"Sorry," she said automatically, placing her camera on the worktable. She hooked a leash to the golden retriever she'd been photographing. "I should have changed."

"You look beautiful," he said with complete sincerity.

Her heart turned somersaults in her chest, a clear reaction to the way his eyes followed her. She smoothed her hands over her wrinkled pants. "You need to get out more." She laughed, trying to lighten the mood.

"Only with you." He stepped toward her, so close she could smell the mix of the shower and his own spicy scent. He uncurled her fingers and took the leash from her, his thumb brushing against the sensitive flesh inside her palm.

"I'll put this one away and meet you out front." He turned and the dog trotted behind him as he left the room.

Lainey rested a hand on the table to steady herself. "He's not playing fair," she murmured to Pita. The dog pricked her ears and cocked her head to one side as she watched Lainey from her dog bed.

Lainey turned off the equipment, quickly applied lip-gloss and gave the dog a quick scratch behind the ears. The puppy, Chip, snuggled in the crook of the older dog's neck. "I'll be back soon, you two. Wish me luck."

Pita's tail thumped twice before she buried her nose under Chip's chubby back end.

Lainey grimaced. "I know. Right?"

Chapter Twelve

Ethan took her to the Pinebrook Inn, a popular upscale restaurant on the edge of town. The time flew by as they talked. Ethan seemed to love hearing about her travels, although he admitted he hadn't even made it to the coast in over a year. This man dedicated to his work and the community was so different from the boy she'd known. It was still hard to wrap her mind around the changes in him.

By the time they headed back to the clinic, her whole body itched with anticipation. She wanted more time with him, as much as she could get. A siren wailed behind them, and Ethan pulled to the side of the road as a fire engine raced past.

"Wonder where they're headed."

Ethan eased back on to the two-lane highway. "Could be…" They watched the fire truck take a right turn at the top of the rise. The road that led to the clinic.

Lainey's blood turned to ice. "You don't think…" Her head thumped against the seat as Ethan slammed his foot on the gas pedal. He turned off the highway and raced along the darkened road as she sent up a string of silent prayers.

Before they got close, a bright light shone through the trees. She rolled down her window, and the acrid scent of smoke leeched into the truck, winding its way through every fiber of her being.

"Oh, no," she whispered as they pulled into the clinic's driveway.

Flames licked the night sky above the shelter. Two fire engines flanked the building, which seemed to glow from within. Huge plumes of smoke soared into the air as firefighters sprayed water from long hoses. Lainey felt mesmerized by the scene, as if watching the whole thing in slow motion.

Ethan's harsh voice broke her reverie. "Call Steph," he ordered, handing Lainey his phone as he parked at the edge of the property. "And stay back."

He jumped out of the truck and headed for the shelter. Obviously, his command only applied to her. Her fingers trembled as she pulled up Steph's number.

After Steph promised to call the other vets and staff, Lainey stepped out of the truck. The air was hot, thick with smoke and tiny ribbons of ash. She walked a few paces in a daze as firefighters ran from the building, cages or animals cradled in their arms.

She saw Ethan near one of the trucks, clearly arguing with Sam Callahan, Brevia's new police chief. He threw up his hands then turned away toward a firefighter holding the leash of the golden retriever she'd photographed earlier.

The gravity of the situation hit her. She was watching her mother's dream—her father's legacy—literally go up in smoke.

"No!" she screamed, although no one heard her over the roar of water gushing from the hoses.

She ran forward, scooping a trembling tabby cat out of the arms of a firefighter.

Ethan was at her side in an instant. "I told you to stay back," he yelled over the noise. "It's too dangerous."

She shook her head, her eyes filling with tears, both from the heavy smoke and pure adrenaline. "We have to help get the animals out."

His mouth pressed into a thin frown, but he nodded. "The fire's in back. We have empty kennels in the clinic and barn. Put the cages in my office."

Without a word, she turned and ran toward the clinic. Back and forth she raced, her chest burning from the smoke and heat. She'd come to know many of the shelter animals and whispered words of comfort between coughing fits.

Soon Steph and one of the other vets arrived, setting up a triage unit in the barn's tack room.

As she moved across the property, a tendril of dread crept up her spine, as if she were forgetting something. She walked into the barn and looked around wildly.

Steph glanced up from where she was cleaning a burn on the leg of a black Lab. "You look like you saw a ghost."

Lainey whipped around and tore back across the lawn toward the shelter. The fire was finally under control, although small towers of flame still rose into the sky at the far end of the building.

Ethan walked toward her, arms outstretched. "The kennels are empty. They're all out."

"Pita," Lainey gasped. "Have you seen Pita and the puppy?"

Ethan glanced to either side. "I'm sure she's here. She wasn't locked up. Probably got spooked and took off into the woods. We'll look for her after—"

"No!" Lainey cut him off. "You don't understand. Chip—the puppy—was shut in my mom's office. I brought him in because Pita spent all day outside his cage in the main kennel. I moved his bed from the studio to the office before we went to dinner. She would've never left him."

Ethan looked over his shoulder at the smoldering building, smoke billowing around it like a blanket. "Vera's office was near the back of the shelter."

He used the past tense. The back of the building looked like a mass of charred kindling. A half dozen firefighters clustered around, still spraying small areas of flames.

She sucked in a shallow breath. "No," she repeated.

"Lainey." Ethan reached for her but she ran full speed toward the building. He caught her against his solid chest. When she fought, he wrapped his arms tight around her.

"Let me go. I need to find her. She's still in there."

"If she's…" His voice was rough against her ear. "Nothing could survive that."

"No!" She flailed her arms, but he pinned them against her sides. She couldn't bring herself to imagine Pita in the office as the walls burned around her. Rage and guilt filled her at the thought of the terror the dog must have felt.

"I can't lose her like this. Please, Ethan," she begged, not sure what she was asking. "Please."

He set her away from him, and her shaking legs were forced to hold her up. "Stay here," he commanded. "I mean it, Lainey."

She wiped the back of her arm across her face. "What are you going to do?"

He didn't answer, just stalked to the shelter's front entrance. At least where the door had been before the fire crew bashed it in to get to the animals.

She saw Sam grab Ethan's arm as he got closer. Ethan said something she couldn't hear, pointing at the shelter then glancing back at her. The two men talked for a moment before Sam took a flashlight from one of the other officers standing nearby. Sam nodded at the young deputy then followed Ethan into the building.

Lainey felt an arm curl around her shoulder.

"Steph called me," Julia said softly. "I got a hold of the hospital and told them not to let Mom know. I'm so sorry."

Lainey's eyes never left the gaping hole where Ethan had disappeared.

"How are you holding up?" Julia tried to draw her away. "Where's Ethan?"

Lainey pointed toward the remains of the shelter. "Pita's still in there. He went after her."

Julia went still. "He couldn't have. That part of the building is about to come down."

As if on cue, a terrible cracking reverberated through the night, and the back of the shelter caved in on itself.

"Ethan!" Lainey screamed and twisted out of Julia's grasp. Her lungs burned from the smoke and from trying to gulp in air. One of the firefighters grabbed her as she ran past. She fought against him, struggling with all her strength.

What had she done? Ethan would have never gone into the shelter if not for her pleas.

"Let me go," she screeched. She kicked and scratched at him, anything she could do to wrestle free.

She saw a shadow out of the corner of her eyes. The firefighter released her and she stumbled forward, landing on one knee, her eyes riveted to the front of the shelter.

From the smoke a figure emerged. Ethan staggered out of the building, cradling Pita in his arms. Two firefighters ran to him. One tried to take Pita, but Ethan didn't let go. Sam Callahan came out a moment later, Chip tucked under one arm. Ethan's gaze crashed into hers.

By the time she got close, a crowd of firefighters and emergency workers surrounded him. Lainey pushed people out of the way and threw her arms around his neck. He held Pita but leaned in close.

"Thank God," she whispered and pressed her mouth against his. She didn't care who saw, didn't think about anything except that he was safe.

She felt Pita shift and looked down. The dog's normally fluffy fur was matted and damp. Patches of red skin showed where fur had burned away.

"My sweet girl." Lainey smoothed debris off the dog's head. "Is she hurt?"

"I don't think so, but I'm worried about smoke inhalation." Ethan bent his head on a round of choking coughs.

"Give her to me," Lainey told him. "You need to be checked by the EMTs."

"I'm fine. Just need water." He coughed again. Lainey knew he'd have to be on his deathbed before he let go of the dog.

"Come on." She took his arm. "Sam, can you bring the puppy?"

"I've got her." Julia answered. She stood next to the police chief, her hand on his back as she cradled Chip to her chest.

Harlan Knox, the fire chief, stepped in front of them as they headed for the clinic. "Next time, Ethan, leave the rescuing to us."

"Will do, Chief."

They walked arm in arm. "Since when did you become such a damn hero?" Lainey asked, her voice thick with emotion.

"Since you needed one," he answered without breaking stride.

She lost her footing for a moment before righting herself. "Is she really okay?" Lainey opened the side door. "She's so still."

Ethan maneuvered Pita onto the examination table in

the back room. The dog tried to lift her head, but the effort seemed too much for her. "It's the smoke that's her problem. The whole place was one black cloud."

A small sob broke from Lainey's lips.

He met her gaze, his eyes serious. "I *will* take care of her."

"I know."

Julia came into the room at that moment, trailed by Steph and the young vet, Paul Thie.

"This puppy is shaking so hard I can hear his teeth rattling."

"Yours would, too, if you'd just been trapped in a burning building." Steph reached for Chip but the little dog clung to Julia for dear life.

"Are you ready to be a dog mom, too?" Steph asked. "He's definitely attached to you."

"I think I'll have my hands full," Julia answered but snuggled Chip closer before pulling him off and handing him to Steph.

Lainey saw Ethan glance at Julia, a small smile curving one side of his mouth. She swallowed hard.

"I'm going to check in with Harlan," she said, her throat raw.

"I'll come with you." Julia turned for the door.

They found the fire chief and Sam huddled together near Sam's police cruiser.

Harlan straightened as the two women walked closer. "Where's Ethan?"

"Taking care of my...of the dog he brought out of the building. What's going on?"

Harlan glanced between Lainey and Julia. "I know what this place means to your mother. I'm sorry, girls."

Lainey nodded, but she could tell there was something he wasn't saying. "Do you know how the fire started?"

Harlan shook his head. "We're trying to figure it out—should know more by morning. Are the animals settled?"

"Almost," Julia answered. "Luckily, none of them were seriously injured."

"It's a good thing your mama had that sprinkler system installed. Tell Ethan I'll come by in the morning." Harlan rubbed his forehead as he surveyed the property. "If he has another place to sleep tonight, that would be good."

"He can stay with me," Lainey said then blushed as she felt three pair of eyes on her. "In the spare bedroom at Vera's." She offered Sam a smile. "Thank you for your help with the puppy."

He nodded. "My pleasure." His gaze strayed to Julia. "Let me know if there's anything else."

Lainey and Julia started back toward the clinic. "I think Harlan knows more than he's letting on." Lainey pushed her hair out of her face.

"Don't go looking for trouble," Julia told her with a level gaze. "It will find you all on its own."

Ethan and Steph were still bent over Pita while the puppy watched intently from his bed in one of the smaller kennels.

"Chip is okay, then?"

Ethan looked up. "When we found them, Pita was lying on top of the puppy, shielding him from most of the debris and heat."

Lainey bent her head close to Pita's face. "You are such a good girl," she whispered. Pita licked at Lainey's tearstained cheek. "He's your baby and you are the best mother."

Emotion threatened to overtake her. She straightened, praying she could hold it together.

Julia cleared her throat. "I'm going to check on everyone in the barn and then head home. Lainey, I'll see Mom in the morning."

"I don't want her to know until we find out how bad it really is."

Julia nodded. "I'll do my best."

"I'll walk out with you." Steph turned to Ethan. "Unless you want me to stay."

He shook his head. "Go home now. Paul and one of the techs said they'd stay overnight. We couldn't have done it without you, Steph."

Steph gave Ethan a quick hug. Lainey saw him wince, but before she could say anything, Steph's arms wrapped around her. "We'll fix this," her friend whispered. "We can make it right again."

Julia started for the door. "Get some rest tonight, you two."

"Thanks, Juls," Ethan answered. "You, too, Steph. For everything."

Lainey rounded on Ethan as soon as they were alone. "You're hurt."

He shrugged. "A few scratches, a couple burns. Nothing major."

"You should have let the EMTs take a look."

"I'm fine. I'll finish here, check on the other animals before I go."

She wanted to argue but didn't. He looked exhausted, but she knew he wasn't going to slow down now.

"I'll be fine at the lake house." He kept his attention focused on Pita. "I don't have to come to your place."

She didn't hesitate. "I want you to."

He met her gaze. "Thank you."

"I should be thanking you." One side of her mouth curved up. "Again."

The puppy whined. Pita tried to stand but Ethan held her steady. "He's okay, Pita."

"Can we take her with us?"

"I think she'll be happier here." Ethan picked Pita up off

the table. The dog shook her head and stretched the leg Ethan had bandaged. She limped over to the kennel with Chip and pushed against the metal gate. "Paul can give her more oxygen if she needs it."

Lainey bent and patted the dog's fur, nuzzling her face into Pita's neck. "You want to be with your baby, don't you?"

Lainey wiped at her wet cheeks and ruffled Pita's fur. Her heart clenched with unfamiliar emotions, emotions she imagined a mother could feel putting her young child on the school bus for the first time or watching years later as that grown child left for college.

"Go on, Pita. Stay with him." She gave a self-deprecating laugh. "He needs you more than I do."

Pita watched her a moment longer then stepped slowly into the kennel. She turned around several times and sank to the floor, her bandaged paw stuck out in front of her. Chip scrambled over her back, tumbling to the front of the cage. Pita barked softly and the puppy waddled back, curling into a ball at her side.

Lainey closed the door to the cage and took several deep breaths before standing. "Maybe we can find a home for them together," she said casually.

When Ethan didn't answer, she glanced over. He stared at her, hands on his hips.

"What?" She slammed shut a cabinet door. "She needs a real family, people who will take care of her." A tremor snaked through her body. "Not let her get stuck in a burning building," she muttered.

"It wasn't your fault." Ethan's arms wrapped around her waist. "She needs you," he whispered into her hair. "Just like I do."

She knew she should pull away. Like the fire had engulfed the shelter, her emotions were stripping away the careful defenses she'd built around her heart, burning down her walls until she was left exposed and vulnerable. Instead, she buried her head against Ethan's neck. "I was so scared," she said, her voice raw. "For you, for Pita—of losing you both."

"I'm here." He smoothed his hands along her back. "I've always been here."

The clinic door banged open and Harlan's voice rang out in the quiet. "Ethan?"

"In the back." Ethan dropped a quick kiss on Lainey's forehead.

She sagged against the desk as Harlan walked into the room. "We've done all we can tonight." He rubbed his thick fingers along his neck. "I'll be here first thing tomorrow. Sam, too."

Lainey's head snapped up. "Why will Sam be back? Do you suspect arson?"

Ethan put his hand on her arm. "We'll talk in the morning. Thanks for everything you did tonight."

She nodded. "Yes, thank you."

Harlan turned for the door. "Night y'all."

When it clicked shut, Lainey glanced at Ethan. "Why did you stop me?"

He trailed his hand down her arm and laced their fingers together. "It's almost midnight. Everyone is exhausted. We'll have time to piece it together in the morning."

"You're right, but I don't understand how this happened."

He tugged her toward the hallway, flipping the lights off as he went. "Say it again." He led her out into the darkness.

"Say what?" The smell of smoke still filled the air, burning her eyes as they walked to his truck.

"That I'm right."

She grinned, amazed he could make her smile even after the night they'd had. "If you want, we can take my car. I'll come back in the morning, too."

He squeezed her hand before letting go. "Let me grab a change of clothes," he said and moved toward the trailer.

For a moment Lainey wondered if she was doing the right thing but pushed her doubts aside. After what they'd just been through, tonight she was following her heart. No matter what.

Chapter Thirteen

Ethan stepped into the stream of hot water and plunged his head under the spray. Dirt and grime slipped away, but nothing could wash off the outright terror of watching the shelter he'd helped build burn before his eyes.

The door to the bathroom opened and he pulled his head out of the water.

"Ethan? Is it okay if I wait in here?" Lainey's voice was hesitant. "The house feels too quiet."

"Sure." He opened the shower door just an inch. She'd changed into a pair of pink-and-yellow polka-dot boxers and matching sleeveless pajama shirt.

"There's room in here for two," he said, then cursed himself. The last thing he wanted to do was scare her off.

To his surprise, she answered with a small, "Okay."

His eyes widened.

"I keep thinking of you and Pita, of the noise from the animals trapped in the building. I changed clothes, brushed my hair. The smoke smell is worse than before."

Ethan wiped his face clear of water and looked at her more closely. Her shoulders shook in an obvious attempt to control her emotions.

"I don't know what's wrong with me." She tried to laugh but it came out as a moan. She bent forward. "I can't…stop… crying," she said between sobs.

He threw wide the shower door and hauled her in, pressing her head into his neck. His back took the brunt of the shower spray to protect her from the streaming water. He whispered words of comfort against the top of her head, using a strength he didn't know he possessed to assure her that everything would be okay.

That he would keep her safe.

Always.

It wasn't a promise he could keep. But he'd say anything to calm her, to stop her tears.

When she'd told him about losing the baby, she hadn't cried. She'd looked more miserable than he could imagine, but her eyes had remained dry. He'd had to walk away so he wouldn't break down in front of her, but she'd remained calm.

They may have stayed together for a few minutes or a half hour. At one point, Ethan reached behind him to adjust the hot water knob. Otherwise, he simply held her, offering his strength and support—hoping this time it would be enough to see her through.

Eventually her body went still, but Ethan didn't move. Not until he felt her head tip. He looked down and saw her eyes focused on an area just below his shoulder.

"You're hurt." Her green eyes transformed to smoky gray.

"A couple of scratches. No big deal."

Pressing her soft mouth to his injury, her fingers spread through the hair on his chest.

His eyes drifted shut as a groan escaped his lips.

Her head rose. "Did I hurt you?"

"That feels…"

She trailed more kisses along his chest and the base of his neck.

"…real good," he finished.

"Ethan?" Her voice hummed along his throat.

"Mmm," was all he could manage.

"I'm wearing my pajamas in the shower." She smiled. She looked so beautiful and sexy, water beading on her face and hair.

"I can help you with that." His hands moved to the front of her and fumbled with the fabric-covered buttons, peeling her shirt off.

When she lifted her hands to her breasts, he pulled them away. "You are incredible."

"You, too," she whispered. Her fingers laced through his wet hair, pushing it off his face. She met his gaze, her eyes heavy with desire. "I want you to know I'm yours."

His lungs expanded so fast it made him dizzy. He knew she meant at this moment. But he hadn't realized until now that those were the words he'd been waiting to hear for the past ten years. Maybe his whole life.

Leaning forward, he kissed her. "First things first," he murmured and picked up a bottle of shampoo.

She made a face and held out her hand. "I still smell like smoke, don't I?"

Instead of handing it to her, he poured the thick, pink liquid into his own palm. "Every single inch of you smells and tastes exactly right." He rubbed his hands together then combed his fingers through her curls.

She groaned with pleasure as he massaged his hands against her scalp. The smell of strawberries and honey filled the small space. Lainey closed her eyes and swayed a little as she tipped back her head to rinse out the shampoo.

She turned her head. "I need you," she said against his mouth, her voice hoarse. She spun and pressed into him, wound her arms around his neck so she could bring him closer. "Now."

In seconds, they were out of the shower and into her bed. They stayed together for hours until every part of Lainey tingled. As she drifted toward sleep, Ethan pulled her closer to him, the heat from his body keeping her warm in the cool of the quiet house as he dropped a kiss on the top of her head.

She sighed and snuggled tighter, feeling more at home in his arms than she had any place else in the world.

The next thing Lainey knew, bright sunlight spilled into the room. She blinked several times, and her eyes focused on Ethan. He was only inches away, staring into her eyes with a quiet intensity that made her heart squeeze.

"Morning," he whispered, one side of his mouth pulling up into a crooked grin.

"Did you sleep?" With her free hand, she tugged on the sheet that covered her from the waist down.

"Some." He drew her hand to his lips, kissing each fingertip. "It was more fun to stay awake and watch you."

"That doesn't sound interesting." She yanked on the sheet again.

"Sleeping, snoring, hogging all the covers…" He grabbed the edge of the sheet and flipped it to the bottom of the bed. "Everything you do fascinates me."

"Hey," she protested. "It's cold in here."

He rolled on top of her, his body giving off more heat than a furnace.

She wriggled her hips then laughed when he moaned. "Shouldn't we get to the clinic?"

"It's early," he said with a hoarse gasp. "We have just enough time."

"For what?" Her hands ran down the corded muscles of his back.

"Let me show you," he answered and covered her mouth with his.

Ethan glanced at Lainey every thirty seconds on the way to the clinic until she begged him to stop.

"Do you think it's a sign?" she asked.

"Of what?"

"I wasn't meant to come back."

"It was a terrible accident. End of story."

He saw her swallow and wished he could convince her. The way Ethan saw it, last night had been a sign that he'd been a bigger idiot than he knew ten years ago. Watching the flames consume the shelter, he'd realized the building didn't matter. The animals had been safe and Lainey was by his side.

He'd let her go too easily that day at the church. Let his pride get in the way of going after her, of convincing her they belonged together. Last night he'd realized if he took care of what was really important in his life, he could handle the other stuff no matter how bad things got.

He pulled down the long driveway leading to the clinic. Cars were parked in the grass on either side. A steady stream of people walked toward the property, stepping off the road to let his truck pass.

Lainey sucked in a breath. "Oh, no."

Several men waved to him. "What are they doing here?" he muttered.

"I wanted to keep this quiet," Lainey said miserably. "Figure out how to fix it before Mama found out."

After parking, he went around to Lainey's side and slipped his fingers into hers.

"Don't do that," she said, tugging her hand back. "It'll just give them more to gossip about."

He didn't release her. "Let them talk."

His gaze was drawn to the shelter building. It was hard to imagine heat and flames engulfing it last night. The stale scent of smoke still clung to the air.

In the back of his mind, Ethan could hear the deafening noise of the building crashing in around him. He forced himself to tune in to the sounds of the morning. Tires crunching over gravel, birds from the surrounding forest.

"They're going to think I'm taking advantage of you." Lainey's eyes were wide and vulnerable.

"I'm a big boy."

One side of her mouth curved up. "Don't I know it," she muttered.

He laughed and pressed his lips to hers, not caring if the whole town watched.

"We're all right," she whispered when he pulled back.

"Oh, yeah," he answered. He walked toward the crowd, ignoring the raised eyebrows and stares several people leveled at him.

"Harlan." He approached the fire chief. "What the hell is going on? This place is a three-ring circus."

"Ain't that the truth." Harlan jerked his head toward the clinic. Ethan and Lainey followed him. "It sure isn't making my job easier."

Ethan ran one hand through his hair and muttered a string of curses. "I've got a solution for that. This is private property—my property." He whirled and started down the porch steps.

"Wait." Lainey's hand on his arm stilled him. She turned to Harlan. "What have you found?"

Harlan shifted uncomfortably from one foot to the other. "Nothing's official yet."

Ethan stepped onto the porch, using his size to tower over the short, balding fire chief. "These people are here because of what you're not telling us."

Harlan rested his hands on his wide hips and pushed back off his heels. "As best we can tell, it started in one of the back rooms. Maybe arson."

"How?" Lainey asked.

"A lamp tipped onto a pile of newspapers."

"My studio," Lainey whispered.

Harlan's tone was all business. "We're still working to determine the sequence of events. But…"

Rage exploded inside Ethan like a cannon. "But what, Harlan? What are you trying to say?"

"You think I did it on purpose." Lainey's voice was achingly quiet and devoid of emotion.

"I think it was a careless mistake." Harlan heaved a weary sigh. "But I've heard mumblings from certain individuals." His eyes settled on Lainey again. "People who've been around for a while—who remember you leaving."

Ethan was numb with disbelief. He stood in shock as Lainey walked to the edge of the porch, her back to him, arms ramrod straight at her side.

He focused on Harlan and spoke through clenched teeth. "That is the biggest load of bull I've ever heard and you know it."

Harlan shrugged. "It's no secret she didn't want to come back. This kind of trouble could derail the event, make it easier for her to leave town again."

Ethan gripped the porch railing. "Lainey put her life on hold to help her mother. She's dealt with more garbage from people around here than anyone deserves. Even if she didn't want to come back, you know she'd never do anything to hurt the animals at the shelter." He shook his head, frustration and anger radiating through every pore.

Harlan held both palms up. "Don't shoot the messenger."

"I'm going after anyone I hear talking smack on her." Ethan pushed one finger into Harlan's meaty chest. "Why don't you send *that* message around?"

"Fine." Harlan waved his hand toward the crowd in the parking lot. "What are you going to do about *them?*"

Ethan took a breath and ran his hands through his hair. "Give me a minute."

With a last look at Lainey, Harlan nodded and walked down the steps toward the shelter.

Lainey turned slowly when Harlan was out of earshot. Her eyes were bright.

"I'm sorry—"

"Were you serious?" she interrupted.

"Hell, yeah. I'll get rid of them all." He'd single-handedly throw every person in this town off the property.

"No." She waved one hand in front of her face. "I mean what you said to Harlan about me. You believe I'm telling the truth?"

"Of course."

"There isn't a hint of doubt in your mind?" She took a step closer, her eyes searching his. "Maybe," she suggested, "I unconsciously want to sabotage the event."

"That's ridiculous." He didn't understand why she was talking crazy but a small voice inside him said it was a test. One he had to pass. "It doesn't matter what anyone says. I know it. I know you."

She launched herself toward him, twining her arms around his neck. "You believe me," she whispered.

Suddenly he was transported back to a Sunday afternoon ten years ago. She'd told him she was pregnant and he'd felt like an avalanche had landed on top of him. He couldn't breathe, couldn't get his bearings in the maelstrom of shock and disbelief.

He hadn't thought she'd done it on purpose. Not until Julia had suggested it at dinner later that night when they'd told their parents.

She'd accused Lainey of trapping him. He'd seen the question in her parents' eyes. For an instant, he'd allowed himself to wonder. She'd looked at him in that moment and he realized now what his doubt had done to her.

He cradled her cheeks between his palms. "I should never have doubted you."

She swallowed hard, and he knew she understood he wasn't talking about today. "It's okay."

"No, it isn't." He placed a soft kiss on her mouth. "I'm sorry. I'll spend as long as you'll let me making it up to you."

He kissed her again. "Let me get rid of these people."

"No." She pulled away from him. "I need everyone together in front of the shelter."

"Are you sure that's a good idea?"

"I have to try to make them understand. Give me a minute to splash cold water on my face."

He studied her but nodded.

Kissing him one last time, she walked into the clinic.

With a deep breath he turned toward the parking lot. "Okay, folks," he shouted. "Listen up…"

Chapter Fourteen

Lainey dug her fingernails into her palms as she walked across the driveway toward the shelter. Maybe the biting pain would help her ignore her pounding heart.

Her mind circled around her last minutes in the office yesterday. She'd turned off the light before leaving, hadn't she? Of course she wanted the event to be a success, no matter the feelings this town brought to the surface in her. She clung to her beliefs as she faced the crowd.

Whispers and murmurs skittered through the group as people spotted her. A volunteer from the shelter reached out as she passed, so numb she barely felt the embrace.

She moved to the front of the large group where Ethan stood with Harlan and Sam Callahan.

The police chief had found her in the clinic just after she'd come out of the bathroom, letting her know the fire had officially been ruled an accident.

"I don't know how the rumors spread so quickly," Sam had said.

"Welcome to life in a small town," she'd answered. Sam had moved from Brooklyn last year, so Lainey knew he still hadn't entirely grasped what life in a community the size of Brevia would mean.

Lainey understood it like the back of her hand. For most of her life, she'd tried to make herself into the kind of girl this town wanted her to be. She'd spent the next chunk running from those arbitrary expectations and her complete failure to meet them.

Today was different. Today she'd move forward on her own terms.

Ethan offered an encouraging smile. "What do you need?"

"I'm good." She tried to return his smile but had a hard time making her lips move. She wanted to relieve some of the palpable tension that hung in the air like heavy fog. "You've… uh…got my butt, right?"

Harlan coughed and Sam turned away as Ethan's eyes widened.

Heat flushed her cheeks. "What?"

His grin spread. "Usually it goes, 'you've got my back.'"

She cringed. "Oops." She felt like a fool but found it easier to smile back at him. "Here goes everything."

She kept her eyes trained on the few friendly faces she spotted.

"Thank you," she began on a squeak then cleared her throat. Although she assumed many in the crowd were here to publically condemn her for any part she played in this tragedy, she was determined to hold her head high. "I can't tell you how much it means to me," she said, her voice ringing out in the sudden quiet, "how much it would mean to my mother to see all of you here today ready to help rebuild what she created."

She saw a couple of older women murmur to one another but continued, "The shelter suffered a terrible tragedy last night. Fire broke out in the room where I've been photographing the animals." She paused for a breath. "For any part I've played in this horrible accident, I'm deeply sorry."

She struggled to remain in control of her emotions. "Miraculously, none of the animals were seriously injured. Something for which Ethan and I—and everyone at the clinic and shelter—will always be grateful." She dabbed her fingers under her eyes. "Several people have suggested the adoption event may not go forward. I'm here to tell you now more than ever, we need to work together to find good homes for our animals."

Confidence blossomed inside her as a number of people nodded. "It will to take time and energy to rebuild, but we're going to keep at it until every single rescue pet has been adopted. My father founded this clinic and my mother has devoted her life to making it a success. I'll give every ounce of my blood, sweat and tears to right this situation. However you feel about me, I hope I can count on each one of you to support my father's memory and my mother's life's work and help us move forward. I know that's what they both would want."

Lainey stopped as applause broke out in the crowd. She glanced at Ethan, who gave her a thumbs-up and was about to continue when Ida Vassler pushed her way to the front. Lainey's stomach plummeted as the old woman came to stand next to her.

"I want you to know," Ida said, her severely outlined eyebrows drawn together, "that I'm personally going to donate twenty thousand dollars to rebuild this shelter."

Lainey gasped.

Ida turned to the crowd and wagged a gnarled finger. "And for any of you boys doing seasonal construction work over in

Gradysville—I'll pay double on the weekends so you drag your lazy cabooses here to get this place up and running."

"I'll volunteer for the foreman job."

Lainey looked out at the sea of faces to where Dave Reynolds, Ethan's best friend from high school, grinned up at her.

"I'm sure the ladies' auxiliary will organize potluck lunches on Saturdays and Sundays," Misty Gragg added.

After that, Lainey lost track of the offers of help and supplies. At least a dozen people came forward to hug her. Many more patted her back and pumped her hand, telling her what a good job she'd done organizing the event, how much the posters with the animal photos were making a difference.

"My sister-in-law all the way down in Pensacola saw it in the paper," one woman told her with a wink. "My husband's family thinks he moved to the sticks up here. Now she wants to drive up and find another cat just so she can say she met you."

"My old sorority sisters down in Charlotte want to meet you, too," Jenny Snyder added.

"Meet me? Why?" It made no sense to Lainey. Her mother was the celebrity.

"They're hoping to convince you to take pictures of their animals. My friend, Pauline, is wild about her Pomeranians."

"They're not the only ones interested in you." Lainey whirled as Julia's voice rang out in the commotion.

Her gaze drifted to the wheelchair Julia pushed.

"Mama," Lainey whispered.

Vera stared back, her expression unreadable. A hush fell over the crowd. In the quiet, Lainey was once again aware of the ruined building behind her and the fact that she was likely the cause of it.

She felt Ethan come to stand beside her. His warm hand pressed into the small of her back. She was eighteen all over again, facing her mother and sister across the dining room table, waiting for their anger to pour out.

"I'm sorry," she said softly, taking a hesitant step forward. "I'm so sorry about the fire. I didn't mean—"

"Come here, child." Although she was unable to walk, Vera's speech was almost back to normal. Despite the wheelchair, Vera looked more like herself outside the hospital room. Pale blond hair framed her face, and Lainey could see the shine of makeup on her cheeks. She bore little resemblance to the frail, sickly woman Lainey had come home to.

Lainey wiped her wet cheeks against her shoulder.

"I'm proud of you," Vera said with a smile.

"But I—"

Vera shook her head, cutting Lainey off mid-sentence. "You've done so much for me, for the shelter, for this whole town." She winked. "If I'd have known what a natural you are, I'd have found a way to get you back here sooner."

"The fire was my fault—"

"The fire was an accident," Vera again interrupted. "Accidents happen." She glanced at the crowd that stood watching the scene unfold. "Carol Dakker, are you here?"

A short, chubby woman with teased hair and an unfortunate yellow tracksuit stepped forward. "What can I do, Vera?"

"Remember when you had too many white wine spritzers after the town council meeting last February and drove Mac's Plymouth through the front window at city hall?"

Carol grew noticeably pale under her bottle-bronzed skin. "There was black ice on the road."

Vera snorted. "It was dry as a bone that winter. Janie Baker?" When no one answered, Vera's voice grew louder. "Don't try to hide, Janie. My daughter parked behind your minivan."

A timid voice spoke from the edge of the group. "Sorry, Mrs. Morgan, I didn't hear you at first."

The crowd parted to reveal a young woman with a mousy brown ponytail, vigorously chewing on one nail. Lainey recognized her as the town's librarian.

Lainey did an inward cringe. As much as she hated being judged, she didn't want to see the rest of the town called to the carpet for past indiscretions. "I think they get the point, Mom," she whispered, straightening. "People are here because they want to help rebuild the shelter. It's okay."

"Always too nice," Vera said with a sigh. "The point is everyone makes mistakes." She raked the crowd with a steely gaze. "My daughter—both my daughters—have done as much as humanly possible to help me. To help all of us."

Lainey made eye contact with her sister over Vera's head.

"Wow," Julia mouthed.

Lainey nodded.

"This event brings in people, publicity and revenue that Brevia desperately needs," Vera continued. "I appreciate those of you who have come forward to help. To the rest of you, what are you waiting for? There's work to be done. Vital work."

She paused for a breath and Lainey noticed her mother's chest rose and fell sharply while her hands trembled.

"Mama, don't wear yourself out," she said, resting a hand on Vera's thin shoulder. She looked out at the crowd. "As I said before, we appreciate the concern each of you has shown for the shelter. We hope we can continue to rely on your support as we rebuild All Creatures to its former glory and beyond."

She heard a noise behind her and turned to see Ethan clapping. Sam and Harlan joined him and pretty soon the entire crowd was awash in applause.

"Find me a handkerchief," her mother said. "I don't want my makeup to run."

Julia dug in her bag and pulled out a tissue as a stream of

people came forward to hug all three of them. Lainey was overwhelmed by the words of kindness and support from people she had thought still hated her.

It took almost forty-five minutes for the crowd to disperse after receiving instructions on how they could each help with the reconstruction that would begin in the morning. Vera was clearly tired by the time Lainey, Julia, Ethan and a few core shelter staff members were left.

"Why did you bring her here?" Lainey whispered to Julia as her mother held court with her staff and Ethan.

Julia rubbed her hands over her belly. "By the time I got to the hospital this morning, she'd found out and was already dressed and ready to go. She'd convinced the hospital director to give her a day pass or whatever you want to call it."

"Is that even legal?"

"Who knows," Julia answered. "Anything's possible with Vera."

"Girls?"

Lainey and Julia both turned.

"I want to see the back of the building."

Lainey heard Julia suck in a breath but Lainey spoke first. "That's not a good idea, Mom. It's pretty awful, and in your condition…"

"Don't tell me what I can and can't do, young lady." She straightened her shoulders. "This is still my operation."

"I didn't say—"

"Ethan, take me to the back," Vera ordered.

He met Lainey's gaze, and she nodded as he stepped forward to take the handles of the wheelchair. "You're the boss," Lainey murmured. "I need to find Sam before he leaves, then I'll be around."

"I saw him head over toward the clinic," Julia answered.

Lainey watched Ethan, Julia and her mother disappear around the side of the shelter then turned. Ray Daniels stood directly in front of her. Lainey's heart thumped. She hadn't seen Ethan's father since her ruined wedding day. He'd hated her then for wrecking Ethan's life, and the steely gleam in his eyes told her not much had changed.

She took an instinctive step back. "Does Ethan know you're here?"

"Hell, yes." Ray smirked at her. "We had a cozy little father-son chat the other night. I even met that fleabag mutt of yours. Petey, right?"

"Pita," she whispered, unease curling around her spine.

"Whatever." Ray moved past her and tipped his head in the shelter's burned-out front door. "Ethan knows who's lookin' out for him around here. I ain't gonna let him be jerked around again."

"You never once looked out for him," she answered, holding fast to her temper. "Ethan hates you, Ray."

"Not as much as he hated you, you little tramp."

His words hit her hard, the brutal truth in them making her stagger a step. "He doesn't…"

Ray flicked his cigarette into the shelter's entrance.

"Don't do that," she snapped.

His ugly laugh filled in the silence. "What's it matter now? You took care of this place real good."

A sudden swelling of resolve stiffened her back. "I didn't start the fire."

"Just like you didn't get knocked up to trap my boy." He leaned closer. "You can't fool ole Ray, honey. I know how bad you wanted Ethan. And I know how bad you wanted to stick it to your mama for turning on you all those years ago. I could help, you know." He laughed again. "Maybe I already did."

She pressed her fingers to the sides of her head. "Shut up, Ray."

"Once a lying skank, always a—"

Something flashed in the corner of Lainey's vision and

Ray slammed into the window to the right of the doorway, shattering the already broken glass.

Tim Reynolds loomed over him then turned to Lainey, the wild gleam in his eyes more frightening then Ray's angry tirade.

Lainey stood absolutely still and forced herself to keep her gaze locked on his. Panic rushed through her as he took a step closer.

"I won't let him hurt you," he murmured, his voice a husky growl. "I won't let anyone hurt you."

"What the hell was that for?" Ray straightened, rubbing his jaw.

"Apologize to her," Tim ordered, still pinning Lainey with his stare.

"It's okay, Tim." Lainey shifted her gaze to Ray. "He doesn't matter."

"Screw you, Reynolds," Ray muttered and spit. "I oughta kick your twerpy—"

Tim lunged forward and pushed Ray into the wall. Tim wasn't a big guy but seemed to have adrenaline fueling him. Lainey shuffled to the edge of the building.

Tim squeezed his hand around Ray's throat. "I said—"

"What's going on here?" Sam Callahan walked across the lawn toward them. "Reynolds, get off him."

Tim glanced over his shoulder, thumped Ray's head hard against the wall and let go.

"Sam," Lainey said on a breath. Relief made her knees weak.

He squeezed her arm. "Is everything okay?"

She gave a slight nod. "Ray…was…just leaving."

Sam eyed Ethan's father. "You, too, Tim."

"I need to talk to Lainey," Tim argued.

She shook her head.

"Not a good idea," Sam answered. "Lainey, why don't

you head back with your mom and Ethan? I'll see these two off the property."

"Thanks, Sam," Lainey whispered. Her legs wobbled, but she darted toward the rear of the building. She didn't want Ethan or her mother to see Ray and Tim.

She had time to get a handle on her raging emotions as Vera barked out to-do lists of things needed to bring the shelter back to life. She didn't get angry, didn't shoot Lainey incriminating looks or make snide comments. It was a good thing because Lainey felt like she was walking an emotional tightrope.

"After what I've been through," Vera said, her tone resigned, "I know you can rebuild anything with enough work."

Lainey let out a pent-up breath. "I'll find another place to have the event—"

"We'll have it here." Her mother's tone was firm.

"She's right," Ethan agreed. "With Dave's help, we can get this cleaned up in the next couple of weeks. Maybe even some framing. I'll move out to the lake house so the trailer can be converted to a kennel. The barn and clinic will hold the overflow animals. It'll be good for people coming to see how we're rebuilding."

Lainey nodded, allowing thoughts of the work ahead to drown out Ray's accusations. "I'll do whatever I can to make this up to you, Mama."

"You already are," her mother said and her eyes drifted shut. "Julia, honey, I think I'm ready to go back."

"Do you want me to take her?" Lainey offered.

Julia cast a meaningful glance toward Ethan, who had walked back toward the shelter. "Take the day off," Julia said with a smile. "I've got it covered."

"Okay," she agreed. "I want to finish a few things here and I'll be over this afternoon."

A quiver near Julia's midsection distracted Lainey. "A

wave just rolled across your stomach," she said in a hushed voice, the movement bringing her totally present.

Julia groaned, but her eyes glowed with humor. "He's like a gymnast—turning somersaults, cartwheels—the whole bit."

They'd been to three Lamaze classes, and Lainey had massaged her sister's shoulders, fed her ice chips and rubbed her feet. But she'd actually touched Julia's belly only a couple of times after the first night.

She reached out a tentative hand. "Can I feel it?"

Julia's mouth curved into a small smile. "Of course."

"He's a strong one," Vera said, rolling her chair closer.

Lainey laid her hand on the soft cotton of Julia's pink T-shirt.

Julia's fingers pressed against hers. "He'll perform better if he knows he's got your attention."

"I don't want to hurt him," Lainey whispered.

"You won't."

Then Lainey felt it. A small thud against her palm. She gasped and spread her fingers across Julia's middle. Three more staccato kicks landed on her palm.

Heartache rose in Lainey like a sudden summer storm. She'd thought she'd felt a few flutters before she'd miscarried and had loved to rub her flat stomach like a lucky Buddha.

The doctor later told her she was probably experiencing indigestion. *Indigestion.* He might have been trying to ease her sorrow but had only succeeded in making her feel like a fool on top of everything else. She couldn't tell the difference between a baby's movement and gas pains. How pathetic was that?

The baby inside of her sister was so vitally alive. Julia's every pore burst with life. Lainey felt like a recovering alcoholic watching someone drink a rare, priceless wine. When alone, she didn't miss what she couldn't have, but seeing someone else enjoy it made her soul ache.

She shook her head, forced her mind to clear. "It won't be long now, buddy," she said to Julia's stomach. "You hold out a few more weeks."

"Longest of my life. Are you ready, Mom?"

Lainey bent and kissed her mother's forehead. "I'll see you later."

Vera placed her hands on Lainey's cheeks. "I'm proud of you," she said.

"Thank you, Mom. For everything." She watched Julia wheel Vera over the grass toward the parking lot.

Ethan placed a hand on the small of her back. "Dave's going to meet me here after lunch to figure out the best way to start rebuilding. Do you want to grab a bite in town or at your place?"

"Do you ever wish you were a dad?" The words whooshed out on a rush of air. When would she learn to leave well enough alone? "I need to understand why you don't have a family. I know you wanted kids."

"That was ten years ago. Wants and needs change." He looked away, began to pace in front of her. "Maybe I said that because I couldn't stand how sad you were after you lost the baby. Look at my old man. He was one helluva role model. Maybe I wasn't meant to be a family man."

She studied him. He was different than Ray in every way possible. "You'd be a great father."

His eyes widened in shock before his mask slammed back into place. "How about you?" he countered. "Why haven't you settled down?"

"My job…" she began.

"That's crazy," he interrupted. "You'd find a way around your work with the right guy."

If only that were possible, she thought. She said simply, "I don't like commitment."

He studied her. "I don't believe you."

"I'm not asking you to."

He rubbed one hand over his face. "We're quite a pair." He walked to her, cupped her face in his palms. "I want to be with *you,* Lainey. Only you."

"Me, too," she whispered and let him draw her closer.

In the quiet, the gentle rhythm of her breath calmed his own heart as her chest rose and fell against his body. The soft breeze played with strands of her hair, tickling his neck as they drifted around him.

"I can't stand to hurt you," he whispered.

"You won't," she murmured.

He wondered how she could be so sure. He'd caused her so much pain years ago. They'd hurt each other.

"I have to move clothes to the lake house. Let's get carry-out and take it out there, away from everyone."

"I can't. I told Ida I'd come over to discuss her donation. That woman has more strings than a circus tent."

"Later then," he said, rubbing his lips across her temple.

"My mom isn't coming home until tomorrow." She almost giggled as she said the words. She felt like a teenager again, but this time she had the boy she'd always wanted. "I could come out for the night."

He lifted her off her feet in a tight hug. "Hell, yeah, you could."

Chapter Fifteen

Rain came down in steady sheets by the time Lainey left Ida's several hours later. She didn't have an umbrella but was too tired to care as the downpour soaked her T-shirt.

She walked into the kitchen—some food, a shower and quick nap high on her to-do list. One good thing about being so exhausted was it made her too tired to think about the extra work she'd have to do to get the event back on track.

Well, almost too tired.

She took a box of cereal from the cabinet and opened the fridge. Between the milk and the orange juice sat a cardboard carton and a plastic salad container.

No note, but an order form was taped to the side of the carton. "Pad Thai, no sprouts, small salad" was written in handwriting she didn't recognize. Pad Thai had been her favorite forever, but she couldn't get it in Brevia. The name of a restaurant from a neighboring town was stamped on the box.

She looked around, not sure what she expected to see.

Would Ethan have driven forty minutes just to get her take-out? A smile spread across her face as she grabbed a fork and dug into the noodles, not bothering to heat them first.

It was the best food she'd ever tasted.

When the phone rang a few minutes later, she picked it up on the first ring. "I can't talk, I'm busy chewing." She laughed into the receiver.

"Lainey? Is that you?"

She recognized the voice and swallowed hard. "Sam?" It wasn't good if the police chief was calling her at home. "Sorry. I thought you were someone else."

"Lainey, listen," he interrupted. "I'm at Memorial North. Your sister's here. They need you to come in…."

"What happened?" Her stomach lurched, the noodles threatening a repeat appearance. "Is she okay? Is it the baby?"

"Car accident. She's all right." He paused. "I'll stay until you get here."

"I'm on my way." She clicked off the phone and reached for her keys.

The rain had turned to a light mist as she pulled on to the highway. She used her cell phone to dial her mother's room but got no answer. Memorial North was situated between Brevia and its closest neighboring town. It was bigger than the local hospital where her mother was but not a critical care center, which reassured her. Anything really serious and Julia would be in Charlotte.

Still her heart thumped wildly as she pushed through the doors under the Emergency Room sign.

She approached the information desk. "Julia Morgan? I'm looking for my sister, Julia."

The woman behind the counter checked the computer. "Exam Three," she answered. "Second door on your left."

Lainey walked quickly down the hall then stopped in front of Julia's room. The steady beep that monitored both Julia's vitals and the baby's heartbeat echoed through the door. She hesitated as memories washed over her.

When she finally stepped into the room, her breath caught. A large bandage covered Julia's forehead above her left eye while a dark purple bruise shadowed the skin underneath. The rest of her face looked pale.

Julia's eyes narrowed when the door opened. "You called her," she said with a moan. "I told you not to call. I'm fine."

Lainey's gaze flicked to the end of the bed. Sam stood there, his arms crossed across his chest, concern and frustration warring in his features.

"You are *not* fine," he told Julia. "Just stubborn."

Lainey watched the two of them stare at each other, wondering if she was interrupting a private moment. Sam turned to her. "She's going to be all right. A few cuts and bruises. The baby's fine. She'll need a ride home. Even if she could drive, her car was totaled."

"Piece of junk," Julia muttered.

Lainey shook her head, frustrated she couldn't follow the conversation. "What happened? Julia, you don't look fine."

"I need to get back to the station," Sam said, glancing at his watch. He placed a hand on Julia's leg. "Let me know when you're ready for something new. I've got a buddy with a used lot over in Ft. Thomas."

Julia rolled her eyes. "I think I can buy a car on my own."

Sam smiled. He stepped over to Lainey. "Go easy on her," he whispered. "She's more shaken than she's letting on."

Julia humphed. "I can hear you."

"Gotta go." With a last glance at Julia, Sam walked out the exam room door.

Lainey's eyebrows rose. "What was that all about?"

"Nothing. That guy may be hot, but he's too much of a stinkin' choir boy for my taste."

Lainey heard the catch in Julia's voice. It scared her more

than she wanted to admit to think of Julia in danger. She'd come to see her sister in a new light since returning, to finally feel connected to her family. She sat on the edge of the bed. "Start at the beginning, Juls."

"It wasn't my fault. It was the rain. And my tires. They should have been changed a thousand miles ago, but I don't have the money. I came around the corner on Whitton's Hill. You know how tight it is?"

Lainey nodded.

"There was a pool of water and the car hydroplaned."

"There's a huge hill on that bend," Lainey interrupted, shocked at the scene Julia described.

"I went over it. The front of the car kind of folded across my lap. Thank God I could reach my purse and my cell phone still worked."

"Did you get a hold of Mom?"

"No." Julia pressed her head against the pillows on the bed and closed her eyes. "She was napping when I left. I didn't want to bother her."

A nurse came into the room, cutting off Lainey's response. She walked to the bed and unhooked the monitor. The room went quiet. "Ms. Morgan, you're free to go. You have a follow-up appointment scheduled. An orderly will wheel you down to the front. Pick up the discharge orders at the desk on your way out." The nurse glanced at Lainey then back to Julia. "Do you have a ride home or should I call a cab?"

"A cab would be—"

"She has a ride," Lainey interrupted and gave her sister's hand a small squeeze. "I'm going to pull the car around to the front."

"Thanks, Lainey." Julia swung her legs over the side of the bed. "I'll be waiting."

Lainey had taken only a few steps down the hall when

Ethan came around a corner, looking as frazzled as she felt. He pulled her into a quick hug then moved back.

"Jake Maguire told me he towed Julia's car, that it was totaled." He struggled to catch his breath. "Is she okay? What about the baby?"

"She's fine. The baby's fine." Lainey resisted the urge to lean into him again. "In fact she's just been released."

"How are *you* doing with all of this?"

She tried to smile but couldn't force her mouth to move in that direction. "Shocked. Relieved. Running on pure adrenaline."

Ethan searched her face, and while she was pale and her eyes tired, she actually seemed to be holding up pretty well given all she'd been through recently. When he'd heard about the accident, he'd worried not only about Julia but also how Lainey would be affected by the possibility of trauma to the baby. He knew a situation like this could bring back memories of the loss they'd shared.

He wanted to wrap his arms around her, reassure her in any way he could, but this wasn't the right time or place. He watched her draw in a slow breath. "Do you want me to stay?" he asked.

Her eyes darkened until the irises were dusky green. She reached up and her cool fingers stroked his cheek. A simple touch from her could send him over the deep end.

She stepped away. "You should go. It'll be easier with the two of us."

He smiled despite his disappointment. "Once a complication, always a complication."

Lainey swayed toward him then straightened. "I know you want to do the right thing. We all do. But this is so new. I'm going to pick up her paperwork and get the car. I'll call you later. Promise." She kissed his cheek and turned toward the nurses' station as he walked away. She didn't glance back, too afraid she'd surrender to the impulse to run after him and melt into his arms.

A nurse came barreling out of the exam room, almost running over Lainey. "Get in there," she barked, hurrying down the hall. "Your sister's gone into labor."

"No," Lainey whispered. In a daze, she returned to the room. Julia met her gaze as another nurse cleaned up a puddle of liquid from the floor next to the bed.

"My water broke," Julia said with an apologetic laugh. "I bent down to pick up a shoe and…"

"It's okay, hon." The nurse straightened, a wad of crumpled towels in one hand.

"I'm not ready. It's not time…the baby…"

The nurse patted Julia's leg. "We'll get you moved up to Maternity and the doctor will see you. Everything will be okay."

"No," Lainey repeated, louder. Her world tilted off-kilter. *Okay. Okay.* That one word haunted her. Stars danced before her eyes and she licked her dry lips.

The nurse turned. "Are you the sister?"

Lainey stared.

"The birth coach, right?"

Lainey forced herself to nod.

"It's a good thing you're here," the nurse told her as she slipped past. "She needs you now."

With the nurse gone, Lainey stepped farther into the room. She opened her mouth to speak, but Julia's face contorted, eyes shut tight as she bit down on her lower lip.

A contraction.

Lainey recognized it but couldn't remember a single thing she'd learned in the birthing classes. Her mind went blank as she watched obvious pain wash through her sister.

As she remembered her own pain.

A moment later Julia's eyes opened again. Her mouth trembled. "Is it really going to be okay?" she asked weakly.

Lainey swallowed and nodded. She used the fear in Julia's eyes to push away her own anxiety. As overwhelmed as she felt, she wouldn't let Julia be alone at this moment. She had a chance now to make something right, once and for all.

She came forward and pushed a sweaty strand of hair off Julia's face, smoothing her fingers across her sister's skin. "We're going to get through this together," she said.

Tears welled in Julia's eyes. "Are you sure? Because—"

"I'm sure. The nurse was right. Everything's going to be okay." She dropped a quick kiss on Julia's forehead. "Better than okay, Juls. You're about to become a mother."

Ethan had walked out of the hospital feeling more alone than he could remember. He'd never been close to his own family.

He'd spent most of his time at the Morgans', happy for Vera to feed and fuss over him. He tried to remember Lainey at that age. She didn't talk to him a lot, always seemed to have her nose buried in a book. Or maybe he just wasn't paying attention.

He picked up Chinese takeout and drove out to the lake house. Flipping on the television, he dropped to the couch, ate and dozed off.

A noise sounded from the floor below several hours later. Ethan stood and wiped his mouth on the back of his sleeve. The last thing he needed was a random bear or raccoons nosing around his trash.

He started down the steps but stopped midway. "Lainey?"

"Hey," she said. "Sorry to show up without calling."

Ethan barely registered her words. Her scent trailed up to him, overriding his senses until he was dizzy with need. He tried to steady his heart, to think of something normal to say. Something to make her stay in Brevia longer than this summer—maybe even forever.

She gave him a questioning look. "If I'm here at a bad time…"

"No," he said quickly. He realized he was blocking her way up the narrow staircase. "Come on up."

He grabbed the remote and flipped off the TV then tried to straighten newspapers and magazines on the coffee table. He picked up his half-empty Chinese carton and moved it to the kitchen counter, next to a stack of crusty dishes.

"I came to say thank you for the pad Thai." She crossed and uncrossed her arms, looking both uncomfortable and adorable. "It's my favorite."

"I remember," he said with a grimace. "I just can't figure out why. Give me good ole kung pao any day."

"That's why I appreciate it so much."

A wave of pleasure washed through him. Funny how doing something nice for her made him feel ridiculously happy.

"I also wanted you know Julia had the baby."

Ethan felt like he'd taken a hard right to the jaw. "What?"

"I went back to the room." Her eyes widened. "Her water broke. Everything went so fast and then—"

He didn't know what to say, how to react. He studied Lainey but couldn't read her expression. "What happened?"

A dazed grin broke across her face. "I have a nephew, Ethan. He was determined to meet the world today. Julia barely had time to push. And Charlie is perfect."

"Named after your dad."

Lainey nodded. "Ten fingers, ten toes. The loudest cry you've ever heard. He's perfect," she repeated in a whisper.

"Congratulations, Aunt Lainey. I'm happy for her. For both of you."

Her head cocked to one side. "Do you ever think about the baby we would have had?"

He stumbled a step.

"If we have a chance," she said with a sigh, "we need to talk about our loss."

His pulse began to thump. He cupped her face in his hands. "I think about that summer—the baby. About what would have happened. About you being my wife." He kissed the tip of her nose. "I only care about our future, Lainey." He forced himself to continue. "Do we have one?"

Her breath caught.

She wanted to answer *yes*. Isn't that why she'd come here in the first place?

She'd meant to drive straight home from the hospital and hide under the covers but instead found herself here. She needed to crawl into the safety of Ethan's arms.

To lose herself in him.

But did they have a future?

This was the time when she should lay everything on the line. Familiar fear rushed through her.

She'd spent so long condemning herself; she couldn't bear to talk about her inability to have children and risk seeing that same judgment in Ethan's eyes. Of being rejected by him again.

Instead of answering, she touched her lips to his. She breathed him in, wrapped her arms around his neck and held on tight.

He didn't disappoint. His kiss was deep, hungry, demanding. Like he was trying to prove something. His desire for her went beyond pure lust or the familiarity of old lovers. He was urgent, desperate and she matched his need.

"You're making me crazy." He laughed into her hair. "I have about as much control as a teenager."

As she drew back and looked deep into his eyes, she had

no doubt that the longing she saw reflected there was only for her.

"Control is overrated," she whispered with a smile.

"I want this forever," he whispered then pressed his mouth against hers before she could answer. "You are the best part of me, Lainey." He led her to his bed as he kissed her forehead, her cheeks, the line of her jaw. "You make me a whole person."

"I love you with every part of me," she whispered. "I always have."

They breathed into each other, melding together until she wasn't sure where he stopped and she began.

She could feel his heart thundering in his chest, matching the pounding of her own. They stayed wrapped tightly together, taking and giving pleasure for hours. When Lainey heard the hiss of sprinklers outside the window, she finally glanced over at the clock.

"It's almost eleven. I should go." Even as she said the words, he nestled her against him.

"Stay."

Little tingles of awareness spread down her spine. "I need to get up early to see Julia before work."

"I'll set the alarm."

She propped her elbows on either side of his chest and looked at him. Could she trust him with her heart again? She was afraid if she had to take another emotional pounding, she might not survive it with her soul intact.

"Please stay with me tonight."

"Yes."

As his mouth claimed hers, her doubts faded away like the moon in the first light of morning. Maybe they were still there waiting to resurface when darkness fell again, but for now his kiss was like the bright sun, warming every part of her.

* * *

Lainey had left Ethan on the lake house's deck with a steaming cup of coffee, a kiss and a promise to meet later that morning.

She'd called her mother on the way to the hospital and after visiting her sister and nephew, she finally pulled herself away and made it to the clinic around noon. She'd called Ethan's cell phone but got voice mail, so left a message she'd pick up sandwiches on the way over.

In a million years, Lainey would have never guessed she'd have such a hard time leaving Julia and Charlie, even for a few hours. But from the moment her new nephew had wrapped his little hand around her finger, she'd been a goner. She hadn't even minded changing his dirty diaper.

Nothing about Charlie or the maternity ward made her revisit her own pain. She stayed totally focused on the present moment, grateful for new life and her chance to be a part of it.

Which may have explained why she'd lost track of time. Vera had called three times. She was being released later that afternoon and was chomping at the bit to meet her grandson. Lainey planned to pick her up when she left the clinic.

As she pulled down the driveway, an ominous feeling settled in her stomach. It was Sunday, but staff from both the clinic and shelter were supposed to be working so they could open on Monday. The parking lot was empty.

She climbed out of the Land Cruiser, holding the takeout bag high as Pita came bounding around the side of the clinic, Chip in hot pursuit.

"Hey, you two." Lainey used her free hand to rub her fingers under Pita's collar then gave the puppy's head a soft pat. "Where is everyone?"

The dogs snuggled together on the dog bed behind the receptionist's desk and she made her way toward Ethan's office, breathing a sigh of relief when she saw his dark head bent over his desk. She pressed a hand to her chest where her heart was beating like mad. Why was she so freaked out?

"This place is like a ghost town," she said as she stepped into the doorway.

"I sent everyone to lunch." He looked up and the anger blazing in his eyes stopped her dead in her tracks.

"What's the matter?" She couldn't imagine anything worse than the fire, but she'd never seen him look that way.

"Why haven't you settled down?" His voice was void of emotion.

She clutched the paper bag tighter against her stomach but kept her gaze level with his. "I told you I don't want that kind of commitment." She forced herself to laugh. "Although now I'm officially a doting aunt."

"Liar." Ethan stood abruptly, sending the chair flying as he leaned on the bookshelf behind him. He felt off balance and didn't know how to right himself. He wanted her to do it for him. Prayed she'd offer a logical explanation. He jabbed one finger at the newspaper spread across his desk. "Tell me the *real* reason you don't want a family."

She stared at him as if he'd lost his mind. "Ethan…"

"How could you have written something like that after everything that happened this summer?"

"Write what?" She leaned over the desk, turning the paper toward herself. Her mouth formed a shocked *oh* as the color drained from her face and her long fingers—the same ones that she'd run across his back hours earlier—dug into the bag she held against her stomach.

He snatched up the newspaper and shook it near her face. "Is this what you were doing at lunch with Tim—having him help you create some sort of manifesto? You got the entire town to trust you and then blamed everyone for how you left. This is how I have to find out the truth of that summer—with your open editorial to the community?" He tried to keep hold of his anger. He couldn't let her see how much she'd hurt him. Again.

Her head shot up. "I didn't write this."

"Who else would have known these details?"

"I don't know."

"Why didn't you tell me?" Ethan paced to the corner of the room and back again. "'Decade-old tragedy shapes photographer's life and career,'" he quoted from the editorial's headline. He'd read the piece so many times he had most of it memorized. "That day in the hospital, after the miscarriage, you knew you couldn't get pregnant again. *You knew.*"

Chapter Sixteen

As Lainey nodded, Ethan felt his stomach hit the ground like a lead balloon. "I told you we could try again and you said nothing."

"I couldn't disappoint you," she whispered.

"Disappoint me?" he bellowed. "How much of a jerk was I? I got you pregnant, you end up infertile and you're worried about *my* disappointment? You didn't even cry. I was about to lose my mind, and you were comforting *me*. All the while knowing you'd never have another chance. Did it ever register that I should have been making *you* feel better?"

"That wasn't how it worked for us." She gave a strangled laugh. "You wouldn't have wanted me without the baby involved. You were fulfilling an obligation and we both knew it."

Why didn't anyone in his life think he was capable of handling something difficult? Was he such an emotional screwup that he couldn't be trusted with anything serious?

He'd thought Lainey saw more in him, but apparently he'd been wrong.

"You were still willing to marry me?" he asked, his voice hoarse.

"It's why I left the church. I couldn't go through with it— like I was tricking you. You had to know, to be able to make the choice of whether you could still be with me. After you got the note, I thought—"

"Stop talking about the note," he shouted. "Your note didn't tell me a thing except that you made a mistake. That being together wasn't worth the trouble it would cause either of us." He crossed his arms over his chest. "It's the same thing now, isn't it? You don't think a relationship with me is worth fighting for."

"I didn't say that." She wiped at her eyes as Pita and the puppy came into the room and crouched at her feet. "And the note…I asked you to meet…you were the one who didn't want me…." Her voice broke off. "You never came."

"Came where? I was at the church for four hours waiting, hoping you'd come back. If I'd meant anything to you, you'd never have left. You'd have stuck it out with me. I didn't care what anyone said. I wanted you."

"But you didn't love me. You never once said it, and I'm sure you didn't feel it."

"What are you talking about? I was standing at the altar."

"Because you felt responsible," she said on a ragged breath. "I wanted you to love me." She paused then added softly, "I still do."

He wanted to tell her that he did, that sometimes when he saw her it felt like his heart was going to burst from how much he loved her. But he didn't. He couldn't say it then, and he wouldn't now. No matter how he felt, she was leaving. She'd made that clear in her editorial. He wasn't going to try to stop her just to be kicked in the teeth one more time.

Pita stretched out her nose and pushed against his hand. His pain was so great he couldn't even take the comfort she offered and he shooed her away.

Lainey's voice cracked. "What if you'd known?" She looked at him, her eyes hollow and desperate. "What if you knew about me then?"

"You never gave me that chance."

"I tried, Ethan." She hitched her chin a notch, as if daring him to contradict her. "What about now?"

He forced himself to look at her, to keep his gaze as hard as his heart. "You didn't trust me, and I can't trust you."

Her shoulders stiffened. "That's not fair."

"Don't talk to me about fair. You've made me a laughing-stock in this town for a second time." He slammed his hand down as anger coursed through him. "You get to waltz in and out of here, but this is my life, Lainey. My home."

She swallowed. "What if I want to be a part of it?"

"It's too late," he told her, his voice icy cold. "I don't want you. We had a good run this summer. I can't make you happy, and I'm not interested in trying. You did me a favor ten years ago, and I'm returning it now."

"That's why you didn't come after me, isn't it? That's why you're doing this now. It's all about you and how much you can't afford to give." The dogs circled her legs as her voice rose.

"Call us even." He forced his mouth into a smug smile. "I guess we both got lucky to figure it out."

She sniffed and rubbed her hands across her cheeks. "Some luck, Ethan."

She turned on her heel and stalked out of his office and probably out of his life for good—Pita and the puppy following in her wake.

After sitting in his office for who knew how long, Ethan

heard noise from the hall, but no one came in, probably afraid of being chewed out.

It had taken him years after Lainey jilted him to walk through Brevia without people looking at him with pity in their eyes. He'd had enough pity to last a lifetime when his mother had run off. The second dose of it had about pushed him over the edge. He'd sworn never to open himself up again. Then Lainey had come back and he hadn't been able to help himself.

He finally came out to oversee a meeting with the staff. He kept the tone light, making sure no one could see the way the pain burned a hole in his stomach.

Checking on the animals and arrangements to open the clinic and shelter the next morning took up most of the afternoon. He was on his way to the lake house when an urgent call forced a detour to the hospital.

He made it to the fourth floor in minutes, taking the stairs three at a time.

"Shh," Julia whispered as he came to a screeching halt at the foot of her bed. "Charlie just fell asleep."

"What's going on, Juls? You said it was an emergency."

Her smile was slightly abashed. "I didn't think you'd come otherwise."

"You're right." Ethan closed his eyes and took a deep breath. "And now I'm leaving before—"

"Don't worry. Lainey took Mom home. She won't be back until I'm discharged tomorrow."

He straightened and studied Julia. She was propped on a collection of pillows, wearing a pajama top with red lips puckering up all over it. In her arms, she cradled a small bundle wrapped in a blue blanket. Ethan could just make out a tuft of dark hair peeking from the center.

He took a hesitant step toward the bed. "That's the baby?"

Her smile widened. "His name is Charlie."

"I know." He peered closer. "Congratulations." Ethan studied the wrinkled, red face that looked more like Yoda from Star Wars than an actual human. "He's…uh…cute."

Julia didn't seem to notice his hesitation. "He's amazing," she said on a sigh.

"Sure." He was out of his element. Kittens and puppies he could handle, real babies not so much. "Julia, why am I here?"

She gazed at him. "You read Lainey's letter in the newspaper?"

"Didn't everyone?"

"What happens now?"

"Lainey and I are through. I won't be taken for another ride." Ethan felt frustration rising inside him and struggled to keep his voice low. "I'm not that much of a fool." He turned for the door.

"Wait."

Something in Julia's tone stopped him. "What?"

"You love her, right?"

"It doesn't matter," he repeated.

"You two were meant to be together. It's the same now as it was ten years ago."

He turned slowly. "Love isn't the answer to everything. You of all people should know that."

She held out the bundle. "Hold him."

His mouth pressed into a thin line. "I don't think—"

"Just for a minute, Ethan. He won't break."

Ethan took the baby from her arms. As delicately as he could, he settled Charlie into the crook of his arm. The baby squirmed and one fist shot into the air. Ethan used two fingers to nudge it back down under the blanket. He was amazed at how soft Charlie's skin felt. At Ethan's touch, the baby opened his eyes for a second, yawned and worked his jaw before settling back down to sleep.

Ethan felt his mouth curl into a smile. Charlie still looked like Yoda, but his magical baby charm was having an effect. "I'm happy for you, Julia," he said without taking his eyes off Charlie.

"This is what she lost."

Ethan's head shot up.

"It wasn't just the miscarriage," Julia continued, her tone soft. "She not only lost that baby, but she knew she would never have the chance again. She was eighteen, Ethan."

"Why didn't she tell me? I could have…"

"What? What could anyone have done for her?" Julia looked out the window. "She listened to everyone telling her how it was for the best—you were both too young. I wasn't the only one who thought she'd trapped you."

"I said we could try again." His eyes drifted shut as he remembered the emptiness in her eyes that day at the hospital.

"Talk about salt in a wound."

"I didn't know."

"Would that have changed things?" Her gaze settled back on him. "Would you have still married her?"

"I did that to her. I owed her."

Julia's smile was sad. "Not exactly the basis for a happy marriage."

"How was I supposed to know if I was in love? It was all so quick and crazy. There wasn't time to figure anything out." He sank down on the edge of the bed, the baby tucked in the crook of his arm. "In my experience, love doesn't count for much. It didn't make things right for my parents. Or for us."

"But what about Lainey?"

"She made me feel whole, Julia. I know it was wrong. You'd just left and she was your sister," he said. He turned, willing her to understand.

"It's okay," she prompted.

"I was happier in those few months with Lainey than I'd ever been before…"

"Or since?"

"Until this summer." He sighed. "It's too late now."

"Come on, Ethan. Hasn't this summer shown you it's never too late?"

Charlie let out a small cry and squirmed. "That's my cue," he said and deposited the baby back into Julia's arms.

"I'm sorry I lured you here under false pretenses," Julia said as she settled Charlie on her shoulder.

"No, you're not."

She grinned. "I don't want to see you mess up again."

"You're one in a million."

"Don't I know it," she said with a laugh. Despite Julia rubbing his back, Charlie's cries got louder. "He needs to eat," she announced. "So unless you want to see my supersized boob—"

Ethan gulped and held up his hands. "I'm leaving." He leaned forward and gave her a quick kiss on the head. "Thanks, Juls."

Outside the closed door of the hospital room, Lainey pulled back as Ethan bent over her sister. With tears almost blinding her, she stumbled down the stairs to the hospital's main entrance. She made it outside and around the corner before her legs gave out. She sank to the concrete, her back pressed against the side of the building.

Her mother had wanted takeout from the Italian deli near the hospital, and Lainey had decided to make a quick stop to see Charlie one more time. She'd peeked into the rectangular window to make sure the new mom and baby weren't asleep.

What she'd seen had almost killed her: Ethan snuggling Charlie while Julia looked on, a serene smile plastered on her face. It was the exact scene she'd pictured for herself. At least until that summer when everything had changed.

So what if Ethan and Julia both told her they didn't have

feelings for each other? Julia needed a daddy for her baby and who better than Ethan to fit the bill?

Once Lainey was gone, it would be only a matter of time before the two of them came together. They belonged together—beautiful, happy, *whole*. She couldn't give Ethan the family he craved.

She should have never come back to Brevia in the first place. She didn't belong here and never would.

With a trembling hand, she balanced on the wall and picked herself up. Taking a tissue out of her purse, she blew her nose hard and started toward the parking lot. She had food to pick up and a life to reclaim.

A life that didn't involve Ethan Daniels.

Four days later, Lainey zipped her oversize duffle bag closed.

"Are you sure about this?" her mother asked from the doorway.

"I have to go, Mom." She sank down on the side of the bed. "The Kittlitz's Murrelet is almost extinct. The fact that they found one with a nest—I can't miss the opportunity to get the photos." Pita nudged her head into Lainey's lap. Her fingers brushed across the dog's soft fur.

"You have to confront Tim. If you didn't write that editorial, who else could it have been? And how did he know about what had happened to you?"

"I'm not sure—the envelope I gave him that day at the church was sealed. It doesn't matter anymore. Maybe Ethan showed him my letter. I was mad at first, but now I don't care." Lainey sighed. "If it was Tim, he did me a favor. Ethan and I could never have made a future together with the past still between us. He doesn't trust me and probably never could. I thought he understood what I did, but he was so angry. I just need to get out of Brevia."

"But you'll be back for the event?" Vera prompted.

"No. I have another assignment." She met her mother's worried gaze. "I left detailed instructions for the staff and volunteers, and I'm going to make the final calls from the airport."

Vera pursed her lips. "What about Pita?"

Tears pricked the back of Lainey's eyes. "It's probably better if I'm not here when she's adopted—"

"Adopted?" Vera's tone turned harsh. "She is *your* dog. You can't desert her."

"That wasn't the deal," Lainey said quietly, too wrung out to offer much of a fight. Pita glanced up and whined. Lainey felt her heart start to crack open and tried to think rationally about the whole situation. "I can't keep a dog with all the travel. It's too much responsibility. I'd only ruin it."

"She needs *you*," Vera repeated. "And she's not the only one."

"I can't do this." Lainey stood, jostling the dog off her lap. She looked at her mother, willing her to understand. "I'm sorry."

Ethan slammed the door to his office and threw a stack of files onto his desk.

He whirled around as the door opened again. "What?" he yelled.

Stephanie Rand ducked as if he'd physically thrown something at her. "What's wrong with you?"

"Nothing."

"Doesn't look like nothing. And the way you've been grumping at everyone the past few days, it sure doesn't sound like nothing."

"We've been swamped." He ran his hands through his hair. "The event's in two days and we've got animals coming out of the woodwork. That's all."

"Have you seen Lainey since the weekend?"

"No," he ground out. "She hasn't been around here."

"Can you blame her?"

He leveled a look at her. "How is this my fault?"

Her lips thinned. "Tim Reynolds is a jerk. I get that he's your friend and you needed to share all that stuff with someone, but for him to publish that junk and pass it off like Lainey wrote it—"

"Hold on a minute." He crossed his arms over his chest. "What makes you think Lainey didn't write it? Tim couldn't have gotten the information from me. I didn't know most of it until I read it in the paper."

"She told me she had nothing to do with it, and I believe her. She has no reason to lie." Steph's eyes narrowed. "And you have a pretty sad memory, Ethan. I saw the note she left the day of the wedding. Maybe she should have told you in person, but she was too scared of your reaction." She leaned back against the door and sighed. "I picked her up at the hotel when you didn't come. She was a total wreck. I think waiting and wondering made it worse for her in the end."

"I'm sick of hearing about the stupid note, Steph." He stepped behind his desk. "I got a half piece of paper with a few typed sentences on it." His eyes drifted shut as he remembered the words that had ruined his life. "'It's not worth it,' she wrote. 'I don't need you and I don't want a life with you.'" His eyes snapped open. "Doesn't get much clearer than that."

Her jaw dropped. "Where did you get the letter that day?" she asked softly.

"Tim brought it to me. She'd left it at the church."

"Her note didn't say that. And she didn't leave it. She gave it to Tim—sealed so no one but you would read it—and asked him to deliver it to you."

He stood, pressure building in his lungs. "What are you talking about?"

"Her note was handwritten, Ethan. I know they had a type-writer in the church office, but she didn't use it. She explained everything about the complications from the miscarriage. She thought you were only marrying her because you'd already committed to it and if she'd told you about her infertility you'd feel responsible for that, too."

"Of course I would have."

"She didn't want that," Steph said, shaking her head. "She didn't want to trap you."

"I made the choice."

"She wanted you to choose her for her, not because of an obligation. She got a room in Charlotte. You were supposed to meet her there. If you didn't come, she'd know you didn't want her."

"That's not what the note *I* read said."

Steph looked confused. "I saw her write it, Ethan. She handed it to Tim. The only explanation is that he typed a different letter and switched them. But why—"

"No!" He pressed his palms on to the desk. It made him sick to think what Lainey must have gone through when she'd left. What she'd believed about him, how alone she'd been. No wonder she'd never settled down. He could imagine how his rejection had haunted her. He didn't know if he could have made it better that day, but he sure as hell would have tried. "Tim left town. I stopped by the paper yesterday. The receptionist told me he went to Atlanta for a few days."

"You guys are—were—friends." Steph shook her head. "I know it was mainly because he's Dave's little brother, but changing the note is plain evil. Why would he have done that?"

Ethan shrugged. "I have no clue, but you better believe I'm going to find out."

"I don't know why Lainey hung out with him," she said, her eyes narrowing. "He always looked at her kind of moony."

Steph paused. "Like the way she looked at you. Maybe he was in love with her the whole time."

"I have to talk to her. She thinks—" Ethan scrubbed his hands over his face. A small glimmer of hope emerged out of the dark shadows of his heart. Lainey hadn't deserted him all those years ago. At least not like he'd thought. She'd wanted him. Maybe she wanted him now....

"She's gone."

"Gone where?"

"She left for Alaska this morning," Steph said apologetically. "She called on her way to the airport. A photo shoot with birds or something."

"The event is this weekend."

Steph lifted her palms in the air. "She told me she worked out the details with Vera before she left and delegated all the outstanding stuff. She's going to have her cell phone with her."

"She ran away again," he muttered.

"Maybe she didn't feel like she had a choice."

He didn't want to hear excuses. "We all have choices. Some people make bad ones." Ethan let disappointment begin to rebuild his defenses. He'd wanted to believe in Lainey. He'd held back his heart, blamed himself for the distance between them. Screw that. She wouldn't stay and fight for their relationship. If that was how little she cared, why should he be any different?

He sank into his chair, forcing his hand steady as he reached for a stack of papers. "I've got to work on these charts."

"I'm sorry, Ethan," Steph whispered and walked out the door.

Chapter Seventeen

Lainey scrambled up the loose rocks on the side of the mountain, deep in the Alaskan wilderness. It had taken her almost twenty-four hours to get to the location, and other than a few hours on the plane between Denver and Anchorage, she hadn't slept since leaving Brevia. Normally, a few minutes in nature were enough to put her in the zone, but she couldn't shake the slightly sick feeling in the pit of her stomach.

She pulled the parka she'd bought in the Denver airport more tightly around her. After the heat and humidity of North Carolina, she felt especially sensitive to the cool, crisp air of the Awapia National Forest.

She waved at Tom Roper, the reporter from *National Geographic* covering the story. He lifted a hand but scowled and continued his cell phone conversation.

"How do you get coverage out here?" she asked as she approached.

He pocketed the phone. "It's satellite." He pressed his fingers to his temples. "Listen, Lainey, I'm sorry to make you come all this way, but I think it's a lost cause."

She looked around. "What's the problem?"

He pointed to a tall pine tree jutting off from a ledge across the valley from where they stood. "Take a look," he said, handing her a pair of binoculars.

She pushed her hair behind her ears and trained the lenses on the pine tree. Adjusting the focus, she studied a medium-sized nest made of twigs and mud midway up the tree and buried deep in the branches. "It'll be a tough shot," she said, lowering the binoculars and scanning the area. "But not impossible. If I can set up near the—"

"It's not the right bird," Tom interrupted.

"What?" She raised the binoculars again. A red-feathered head peeked out of the nest. "It looks like the pictures you faxed me."

Tom shook his head. "The bird is right. The babies aren't."

"I don't get it."

"The story was the Murrelet, which is on the verge of extinction, having a nest full of eggs."

"Right," she agreed, not following his logic.

He grabbed a book from on top of the backpack that sat near his tent opening. "This is its nest." He pointed to a picture of an oval-shaped mass of leaves and grass. "That," he said, inclining his head toward the pine tree, "is a warbler's nest with baby warblers in it."

She squinted against the bright sunlight and stared at the tree. "Then why is a Kittlitz's Murrelet with the wrong baby birds?"

"Apparently, birdbrained isn't just a figure of speech. The stupid Murrelet doesn't seem to know it's not hers."

"Where's the warbler?"

"Who knows?" He shrugged. "Fox food probably. But that

Murrelet isn't going to help population issues by feeding war-bler chicks. Those birds are a dime a dozen up here."

Lainey raised the binoculars again and focused on the pine tree. The nest looked empty until a flash of red came into view. The Murrelet landed on the edge with a small insect clamped in its beak. Three tiny brown and white heads poked up, all clamoring for the morsel. The Murrelet dropped the insect into one waiting beak and took off again.

Lainey's mouth went dry and her skin tingled. "That's the story."

Tom stared at her. "There is no story."

"How many times do you find deserted nests?"

"Enough."

"How many times do you see an animal or bird adopting orphaned babies?"

He shaded his eyes and turned toward the pine tree. "You don't."

"But we are." Lainey pulled her backpack off and dug through it for her camera. "I don't know why the Murrelet isn't laying her own eggs." She attached a telephoto lens to the end of her camera. "But I can tell you it's amazing to watch that bird's determination to have a family of her own. It's a miracle. And I'm not the only one who will think it."

Tom nodded slowly. "I get it."

Lainey sighed. "Me, too. Finally."

By the time Ethan pulled his truck into the driveway at the lake house, it was close to midnight. The adoption fair was tomorrow, and he'd spent every waking hour for the past few days at the shelter getting things ready. He knew the event would be a success by the phone calls and emails they'd already received from people interested in adopting. He also knew that Lainey deserved most of the credit for the way she'd organized volunteers and publicized the event.

The anger that had crowded out every other emotion when he'd discovered she'd left again had been replaced by a dull ache in his chest whenever he thought of her. She'd once again become the North Star in his life, and the pain of losing her was no easier to bear the second time around. Especially knowing it could have been different ten years ago and wondering if he could have changed the outcome this summer.

Even his dream home seemed empty without her in it. That first night, he'd come close to throwing every piece of furniture into a huge bonfire when her smell seemed to linger in each room. As if he could burn away her memory.

He climbed the front porch steps slowly then noticed that the door stood wide open. It was one thing to joke about burning his stuff, another to have it stolen. He raced into the house but stopped short at the sight of a cigarette glowing in the darkness. "Dad," he murmured.

"I hope you don't mind I stopped by to check out the new pad." Ray took a pull from his beer bottle. "I have to admit you did a pretty fine job with it."

Ethan dropped his keys to the coffee table and crossed his arms over his chest. A run in with his father was the last thing he needed. "Couldn't resist a good gloat?"

Ray flashed a self-satisfied grin. "I'm not one to say I told you so, but—"

"Save it." Ethan turned toward the kitchen. He hadn't eaten since having a Pop-Tart this morning. "I've got a big day tomorrow and need some sleep."

"What's Lainey's connection with Tim Reynolds?"

Ethan pulled a carton of leftover kung pao out of the fridge. "They went to high school together. I don't know. Isn't Brevia one big screwed up family at the core?"

"Why do you think she told him all that stuff?"

"*I* don't think she did."

Ray gave a gruff laugh. "I can't see you laying your soul bare to Dave's twerpy little brother."

"I guess Tim switched the note Lainey left for me for a different one, the one I actually read." Ethan scrubbed his palm across his face. "What's it matter now?"

"It might if you knew the whole story. I'm heading down to Florida in a couple of days. Maybe you want to help your old man out with some gas money? I can make it worth your while."

Ethan hissed out an angry breath. "The only time I see you is when you need something, Dad. I'm done being used. By anyone."

"You may not feel that way if you hear me out. How much do you remember about Dave and Tim's mother?"

Ethan turned, fork in midair. "She was kind of a train wreck. Drank a lot, string of loser boyfriends after their dad left town." His eyes narrowed as unease pricked his spine. "Why?"

"Diane Reynolds was a firecracker in her day. She waitressed at the bar where a few of us hung out. Right about the time she and her husband separated and your mom and I were on the skids. Things happened."

"What kind of things?"

Ray wiggled his heavy eyebrows. "Crazy things, son." He whistled low. "Like I said, she was a firecracker."

"You cheated on Mom with Dave's mother?"

"Your mother was one foot out the door already."

"I thought she left because being a mother was too much to handle. You let me believe it was my fault."

Ray shrugged. "Who knows what would have happened if it had just been the two of us. We had some good times at the beginning, your mom and me."

Ethan tossed his food into the garbage can and the fork into the sink, his appetite gone. He'd spent years believing that he was the reason his mother had deserted them. It had shaped so much of who he was—his inability to trust people, to be vulnerable. He'd never wanted to risk that kind of pain again.

"Does Dave know?" How could his best friend of almost two decades not tell him something like this?

"I don't think so," Ray said then grimaced. "Tim is another story. He walked in on us along with his dad. I guess there had been talk of a reconciliation, but our little deal ended it. Diane made him promise not to tell you or Dave. I guess he kept his word. The divorce went through right after that."

Ethan felt his jaw drop. "No wonder Tim hated me. All those years of pretending things were fine when he knew you'd destroyed his family."

Ray jumped to his feet. "Destroy is a mighty strong word, Ethan."

"That's what you did. You destroyed their family and in turn, Tim took his revenge on me. And Lainey got hurt in the process."

"I didn't think—"

"That's always been your problem, but it doesn't fly as an excuse." Ethan felt his world tilt. All those things he'd never said, he'd never let himself feel...

He took a step toward his father and pointed to the front door. "I'm not giving you a penny tonight or ever again. Leave. Now. And this time don't come back."

"I'm helping you here. I didn't have to do this. You're picking a skirt over your own flesh and blood?" Ray asked as he walked to the door, his voice a little desperate. "Think about it, son."

"We're done, Ray. No more unexpected visits, no more phone calls when you're between jobs. We're done." Ethan slammed the door on his father with no regrets.

* * *

Lainey parked her rental car almost a quarter-mile down the road from the shelter then walked with a steady stream of people headed for the adoption fair.

Stopping midstride, her heart filled as families and couples came down the driveway leading dogs or holding cardboard boxes with new pets they were taking home. She recognized some of the animals, and while it was bittersweet to see the ones she'd come to love leaving, her heart swelled to see them going to true homes.

She'd been so scarred by the miscarriage and its aftermath, she'd believed she wasn't worthy of the role she wanted most in the world. But biology didn't make a person a mother or create a family—only love could do that. There were many, many children in the world who needed homes, who needed the love that Lainey now knew she could give.

"Lainey!"

She turned at the sound of her name.

"I knew you'd come back," her mother said, still limping as she hurried across the yard while Julia followed behind. "Do you know we've doubled the amount of adoptions from last year?"

Lainey turned to her sister. "Where's Charlie?"

"He's napping in the shelter office. Ida Vassler's with him. Turns out the old battle-ax has a soft spot for babies."

"Do you feel okay, Mom?" Lainey asked. "You're not over-doing it?"

"I feel better than I have in years. This is exactly what your father would have wanted to see." Vera took a deep breath. "It's all because of your work."

Lainey glanced at Julia. "Everyone pitched in to make it a success. The shelter and clinic staff, Julia, Ethan…" Her voice trailed off.

"What happened in Alaska?" her mother asked softly.

Lainey's throat clogged with emotion, but she only shrugged. "The usual. I took some pictures, met with—"

"What really happened?" Julia interrupted. "When you left, it didn't seem like you'd be back at all, let alone for the event. Your message yesterday only said you'd be here and we needed to talk. I imagine there's a pretty good reason."

It had been a whirlwind week, and Lainey was running on pure adrenaline at this point. Not exactly the clear mind-set in which she'd prefer to have this conversation. But one thing she knew for certain: no more running away. She'd face whatever challenges life threw at her head-on with no regrets. She swallowed and began, "I want to apologize to you both."

Her mother waved a hand. "We're moving forward, Mela-nie. No need—"

"Mama." She wrapped her hand around Vera's fingers and squeezed softly. "There is a need. I need to say this." She looked at her sister. "To both of you."

Julia nodded. "Go ahead, Lain."

"First off, I'm not sorry I fell in love with Ethan or about my time with him. If I could have picked a different man I would have. But that's not how the heart works." She took a breath. "What I *am* sorry for, Mama, is that I felt inferior to Julia and was so scared of disappointing you and Daddy that I didn't stick it out and make things better back then. I always thought I was the odd girl out. I didn't measure up to you or Juls and what a woman should be—"

"That's ridiculous, Lainey." Her mother shook her head. "You—"

Vera stopped as Julia clapped a hand over her mouth. "Let her talk, Mama. For once in your life, let someone else finish a thought." She kept her hand over Vera's mouth until their mother finally nodded. Julia flashed a self-congratulatory smile at Lainey. "Continue, please."

That tiny moment of levity made all the difference to

Lainey. These women were her family, and she could tell them everything she'd needed to say for so long. "After I lost the baby, the doctor told me about the scarring and how it meant I wouldn't be able to get pregnant again. It pushed me over the edge. I already thought I didn't deserve Ethan, and it was like the universe giving me a sign that I was so messed up I wasn't even fit to be a mother."

Tears welled in her mother's eyes.

"I should have told you," Lainey said quickly before Vera could speak. "I was ashamed of who I was, and it felt like part of my punishment should be to carry the burden alone. By the time the wedding day came, I knew I couldn't keep the secret from Ethan. But it felt like if I said the words out loud it would make it too real. So I left the note. It was cowardly, and I don't blame him for his reaction to it then or now."

Julia took a step forward. "Ethan never read your note, Lainey. Tim Reynolds switched yours for a couple of lines about you wanting to end things."

"What?" Lainey whispered as her jaw dropped. "Why?"

"I'm not totally sure, but you need to know Ethan didn't desert you the way you thought."

Lainey tried for a moment to wrap her mind around that concept then shook her head. "It doesn't change the facts. *I deserted him.* All of you. If I'd had the courage to face him on our wedding day, there wouldn't have been any confusion. I don't know if I deserve a second chance with Ethan after what I put him through, but I owe him an honest conversation about my feelings then and now. Like you said, Mama, it's time to move on. Whether or not I can have children biologically doesn't make me damaged goods. I've let my sorrow define me for too long. I'm making a change starting today. I want a family, and I'm going to have one. I want both of you and Charlie to be a part of my life. This summer has shown how much you mean to me and how lonely I've been. I just hope it's not too late."

She looked at Julia who smiled then pulled her into a hug. "I have a lot to make up for, too, little sister. We'll be all right. Charlie needs his favorite auntie to spoil him rotten."

"Absolutely," Lainey agreed.

They both turned to Vera.

"Am I allowed to speak now?" she asked with a small smile.

Lainey grimaced. "Of course."

Her mother took both Lainey's hands in her own. "I'm proud of you, Lainey. For what you did this summer and the changes you're making. If my stroke is what brought you back here, then I'm thankful something good could come from it. You'll be a wonderful mother." She paused and wiped at her eyes then added, "I want lots of grandkids."

The three women hugged as more families with dogs trailed by them. Lainey heard her name spoken and looked up to see Tim standing near the clinic's entrance.

"How dare he show up here," Vera whispered on a hiss of breath.

Julia's shoulders stiffened. "I'll kick his butt into next week."

She took a step toward Tim but Lainey tugged her back. "I should talk to him. I need to know what happened at the wedding and why he published all that garbage under my name."

"All you need to know is he's a scumbag," Julia argued.

"He's part of this. Another challenge and I'm going to face it."

Julia studied her then nodded. "Come on, Mama. We'll check on things at the shelter. Lainey, we're right around the corner if you need anything."

"Your sister can be kind of scary when she wants to," Tim said when they'd gone.

"She wants to protect me."

"Since when?" he answered with a scoff. "We were alike—no one in our corner. The way I remember it, the only person who protected you was me."

Lainey frowned. "Is that what you call switching the note, Tim? The editorial exposing my personal business for everyone to read? That's exploitation, not protection. I came back here to make amends, not more enemies."

He took a step closer to her, running one hand through his thinning hair. "Don't you understand? I did those things for your own good. You need to get out of this town. You're better than Brevia. Definitely better than Ethan Daniels. He's just like his father."

"Ethan is nothing like his father, which is not the point. You had no right to interfere in my life."

"I did it because I loved you. I still do. If you hadn't been so obsessed with Ethan, maybe you would have noticed. I hated to see how sad you were when he hurt you. It made me crazy when everyone in town turned on you. I'd never do that, Lainey. We want the same things in life. I could travel with you. We'd see the world together if you'd only give me a chance."

He reached out and Lainey took a step away. What he'd done was wrong and unforgivable. "You don't show you love someone by manipulating them, Tim." She crossed her arms over her chest. "I thought we were friends. I trusted you. You abused my trust in the worst way possible. Not to mention the pain you caused Ethan and the rest of my family. There is no chance for us and there never was. Whether or not Ethan is in the picture doesn't change that. Stay away from me and out of my life, once and for all."

His jaw dropped. "You can't mean it."

She started up the clinic steps. "I have nothing more to say to you, Tim," she called over her shoulder.

She made it to the front porch just as Tim grabbed her arm. "Let me explain," he yelled, yanking her back. "I can make you understand."

As she tried to pull away, her shoe caught on the last step and she tumbled into him. "Get your hands off me," she hollered as his arms wrapped around her, too angry to care about the small crowd of people that had gathered in the front driveway to watch the spectacle.

"Please, Lainey—"

"Let her go, Reynolds."

Lainey caught a glimpse of Ethan filling the doorway of the clinic just before Tim pushed her away. Off balance, she dropped onto all fours in the grass.

"Stay out of this, Ethan. It's between Lainey and me." Tim's voice sounded petulant.

"There is nothing between the two of us," she snapped, standing up then grimacing as she tried to put weight on her ankle.

Ethan's gaze met hers, and she could see him read the pain in her eyes. In an instant he was in front of Tim, practically lifting him off the ground by his shirt collar. "If you've hurt her, I'm going to—"

"It's okay," she said quickly, placing a hand on Ethan's chest. The last thing any of them needed was another public scene.

"Tim, what the hell is wrong with you?" Dave Reynolds elbowed his way through the cluster of people.

Ethan gave Tim a solid shove then came to stand next to Lainey. "Get him out of here, Dave."

Tim swatted at his brother's hand. "You think he's your best friend, Dave. But you don't know the things I do. What his old man did. Ethan isn't so high-and-mighty. He's cut from the same cloth."

"I do know," Dave said, temper flaring in his eyes. "I know

about Ray and our mom. It wasn't Ethan's fault. We were all kids when it happened."

"Everyone knows his mother left town because she didn't want to be saddled with a family. If it wasn't for Ethan, maybe his dad wouldn't have come sniffin' around Mom. Maybe she and Dad—"

"You need to shut your trap." Dave grabbed the back of Tim's neck and pulled him through the crowd. "Before I do it for you." He looked toward Ethan. "I'm sorry, man. About everything."

Ethan gave him a small nod.

"You too, Lainey. I wish I could make it up to you."

She swallowed and tried to offer a reassuring smile. "It's okay, Dave."

"Show's over, folks," Ethan called out as Dave disappeared into the crowd. "Nothing more to see here." He looked down at Lainey, his eyes dark. "We need to talk."

She nodded then winced as she put weight on her ankle.

"You're hurt."

"It's fine," she said quickly. "Just twisted it a little."

Ethan cursed under his breath and gathered her into his arms. He climbed the steps of the clinic and maneuvered inside, not putting her down until the door was safely closed and they were alone.

"I know you probably hate me more now," she said quietly, focusing her gaze on a place just past his shoulder. "The things Tim published in my name were awful, and instead of facing the problem, I ran off again. I'm sorry I didn't stay, then and now. I was wrong—"

He covered her mouth with his, cutting off the rest of her sentence. A sliver of hope began to grow in her, blooming into something more when she pulled back and met his gaze. She saw the same love shining in his eyes she knew was reflected in her own.

"You don't hate me?"

"I could never hate you." He smoothed his palms over her cheeks. "As much as I wanted to—tried to—I've always loved you, Lainey. All those years you were gone, it was like you'd taken a part of my soul with you." He pressed another kiss to her mouth. "I'm half a man without you. You make me whole."

"The infertility made me feel like part of me was missing. Even you couldn't fill the empty space. How could I expect you to accept me when I wouldn't accept myself? I know I can't give you the family you've wanted—"

He shook his head. "What I want is you. You're all I've ever wanted."

His words made her heart soar. "I want you, too, Ethan. I want us to have a family. Together." She paused to catch her breath as emotion clogged her throat. "I should have talked to you earlier, been honest from the start. I love you so much. I can't imagine my life without you in it."

"You never have to." He pulled her down the hall toward his office. "I want to show you something."

She leaned on him as they walked, his fingers warm and sure laced in hers. He picked up a stack of papers from his desk and handed it to her.

Her eyes widened as she looked over the brochures and books on adoption. She jerked her head up. "You'd be willing to consider adoption?"

He smiled and pulled out a slip of paper with a boarding pass printed on it. "I was leaving for Alaska tonight. I let you get away once and didn't plan to repeat that mistake. It doesn't matter to me whether you give birth or we find a child who needs us as much as we need him or her. I want to see you hold our child in your arms, Lainey. I want to grow old with you, take our grandkids to Disney World. I want a life with you."

"I was such a fool." She struggled to catch her breath. "For so long I thought I was being punished—I didn't deserve to be a mother." When he reached for her she shook her head. "It was an accident, Ethan. I realized that in Alaska. I finally understood my life is what I make of it, not something that happens to me." She smiled through her tears. "And I want to make a life with you."

He drew her to him and caressed her mouth with his. She gave herself up to the pleasure of his touch until a thought pierced the edge of her mind.

"Oh, no!" she yelled, pulling back.

His eyes were dark as he looked at her. "What is it?"

"Pita," she whispered. "I told Mom to put her on the adoptive animal roster. And the puppy, too. I thought they'd be better without me, but I need them. Pita and Chip belong to me. To us." She whirled for the door. "What if they're already gone? I have to get them back, Ethan."

He grabbed her arm. "Come on."

Instead of turning toward the front, he led her down the hall to the back. "There's no time, Ethan. I need to—"

He opened the door to one of the empty exam rooms and flipped on the light switch. Pita trotted out with Chip trailing behind her and sniffed at Ethan.

Lainey gasped and the dog charged at her, tail wagging in an ecstatic greeting. She dropped to the ground and wrapped her arms around Pita's neck while the puppy dashed over to cover her with enthusiastic kisses.

"I never put them with the other animals. They're yours, sweetheart. Always have been."

Straightening, she hugged him as Pita and Chip pranced around them, yipping wildly. "Just like you?" She rained kisses across his face.

"Just like me," he agreed. "You're still the one, Lainey. You always will be."

She sighed and rested her head on his chest. "Are you sure you're ready for this?"

"I've been waiting for this moment for ten years."

"Better or worse, Ethan. I'm here for good. Forever."

His mouth grazed over hers. "Forever," he agreed.

She'd found her place in the world and couldn't imagine belonging anywhere else. She lost herself in his kiss once more, knowing she was finally home.

* * * * *

#2245 ONE LESS LONELY COWBOY
Kathleen Eagle

Cowboy Jack McKenzie has a checkered past, but when rancher's daughter Lily reluctantly visits her father, he wants more than anything to show that he's a reformed man. Has she made up her mind too early that this would be a short stay at the ranch?

#2246 A SMALL FORTUNE
The Fortunes of Texas: Southern Invasion
Marie Ferrarella

After a broken marriage, Asher Fortune moves to Red Rock, where he needs someone to help him and his four-year-old son, Jace, start a new life. He knew upon their first meeting that Marnie was great for Jace, but he didn't realize what was in store for *him!*

#2247 HOW TO CATCH A PRINCE
Royal Babies
Leanne Banks

Hardworking Maxwell Carter has just found out he's the son of the ruling prince of Chantaine, and he's been convinced by his dependable assistant, Sophie, to visit his newfound family. They see the potential sparks between the two immediately, but can a royal makeover by his half sisters help this plain Jane catch the prince's heart for good?

#2248 THE RIGHT TWIN
Gina Wilkins

Aaron Walker retreats to the Bell Resort to escape the pressure of his overachieving family's expectations, only to find his highly successful twin already there, stealing the spotlight as usual! But the beautiful Shelby Bell has eyes only for the restless and shy twin, and will do what it takes to convince him that she is exactly what he has been looking for all his life.

#2249 TAMMY AND THE DOCTOR
Byrds of a Feather
Judy Duarte

Cowgirl Tammy Byrd has always been a tomboy, outroping and outriding all the men on the ranch. Until Dr. Mike Sanchez presents her with a whole new challenge that doesn't involve getting her hands dirty. Can she learn to let her hair down—and lasso the man of her dreams?

#2250 DADDY SAYS, "I DO!"
The Pirelli Brothers
Stacy Connelly

When Kara Starling takes her nephew to meet the father he's never known, she doesn't expect Sam Pirelli to be the perfect daddy. And she certainly never guessed that he could also be the perfect man for her!

REQUEST YOUR FREE BOOKS!

2 FREE NOVELS PLUS 2 FREE GIFTS!

✦HARLEQUIN®

SPECIAL EDITION

Life, Love & Family

YES! Please send me 2 FREE Harlequin® Special Edition novels and my 2 FREE gifts (gifts are worth about $10). After receiving them, if I don't wish to receive any more books, I can return the shipping statement marked "cancel." If I don't cancel, I will receive 6 brand-new novels every month and be billed just $4.49 per book in the U.S. or $5.24 per book in Canada. That's a savings of at least 14% off the cover price! It's quite a bargain! Shipping and handling is just 50¢ per book in the U.S. and 75¢ per book in Canada.* I understand that accepting the 2 free books and gifts places me under no obligation to buy anything. I can always return a shipment and cancel at any time. Even if I never buy another book, the two free books and gifts are mine to keep forever.

235/335 HDN FVTV

Name	(PLEASE PRINT)

Address	Apt. #

City	State/Prov.	Zip/Postal Code

Signature (if under 18, a parent or guardian must sign)

Mail to the **Harlequin® Reader Service:**
IN U.S.A.: P.O. Box 1867, Buffalo, NY 14240-1867
IN CANADA: P.O. Box 609, Fort Erie, Ontario L2A 5X3

Want to try two free books from another line?
Call 1-800-873-8635 or visit www.ReaderService.com

* Terms and prices subject to change without notice. Prices do not include applicable taxes. Sales tax applicable in N.Y. Canadian residents will be charged applicable taxes. Offer not valid in Quebec. This offer is limited to one order per household. Not valid for current subscribers to Harlequin Special Edition books. All orders subject to credit approval. Credit or debit balances in a customer's account(s) may be offset by any other outstanding balance owed by or to the customer. Please allow 4 to 6 weeks for delivery. Offer available while quantities last.

Your Privacy—The Harlequin® Reader Service is committed to protecting your privacy. Our Privacy Policy is available online at www.ReaderService.com or upon request from the Harlequin Reader Service.

We make a portion of our mailing list available to reputable third parties that offer products we believe may interest you. If you prefer that we not exchange your name with third parties, or if you wish to clarify or modify your communication preferences, please visit us at www.ReaderService.com/consumerschoice or write to us at Harlequin Reader Service Preference Service, P.O. Box 9062, Buffalo, NY 14269. Include your complete name and address.

SPECIAL EDITION

Life, Love and Family

Look for the next book in
The Fortunes of Texas: Southern Invasion miniseries!

After a broken marriage, Asher Fortune moves to
Red Rock, where he needs someone to help him
and his four-year-old son, Jace, start a new life.
He knew upon their first meeting that Marnie was
great for Jace, but he didn't realize what was in
store for *him!*

A Small Fortune
by *USA TODAY* bestselling author
Marie Ferrarella

*Available March 2013 from Harlequin Special Edition
wherever books are sold.*